Wholly Ghost

Stories

Robert Subiaga, Jr.

WHOLLY GHOST

All persons, places, and organizations in this book—except those clearly in the public domain—are fictitious; and any resemblance to actual persons, places, or organizations living, dead, or defunct is purely coincidental. This is a work of fiction.

Xaos Books are published in the United States by Chaos Warrior Productions

Library of Congress Cataloging-in-Publication Data

Subiaga, Robert Jr., 1965

Wholly Ghost / Robert Subiaga, Jr.

p.   cm.

ISBN 978-1-884759-86-4

I. Title.

First Printing

1 2 3 4 5 6 7 8 9

PUBLISHED IN THE

UNITED STATES OF AMERICA

For my maternal grandfather

And my paternal grandmother

who always gave me the feeling I had a place

to be

Contents

THE ARTIFICE OF RESPIRATION

Quentin flipped the switch and fluorescence banished the darkness, but not the emptiness. The medical examiner's laboratory was a tomb, after all, albeit a well-scrubbed and sanitized one. And Quentin immediately decided, for the first time ever, to forgo his usual pot of coffee. Caffeine would do nothing for this kind of lethargy.

"Quentin E. Devereaux, at your service," he called out mechanically, knowing only his own echo would reply. "Quentin E. Devereaux," he added in a voice softer, but hinting at more real emotion. "Q.E.D."

Quentin used his fingers to comb back the thin hair, blond enough to be near-white, that lay, flat and oily, on his oversized head. He lathered with specialized soap over the lab's stainless steel sink and scrubbed his hands until they were as raw as they were sterile, then donned protective goggles, latex gloves, and a disposable smock, to protect him from the inevitable flecks of blood, of mucus, of flesh.

"The oldest adage in medicine is about pathologists," he said to the draped bodies. "We have all the answers. We're just always too late." The corpses said nothing in reply, even though this was approximately the four-thousandth time Quent had repeated the joke. But then, perhaps these bodies had never heard it. Quentin never had repeat customers.

Quentin scowled. "You are entering the most fascinating sphere of police work—the world of forensic medicine," he said, trying his best, in vain, to sound like Jack Klugman on the old TV show, "Quincy." Quincy, who solved murder on a regular basis in the course of conducting his job; Quincy, who seemed so warm and lovable because everyone knew he did not merely doctor *corpses*. Quincy, everyone knew, *cared*.

Quentin had experienced only disappointed frowns thrown his way. They came most often when he went beyond stating he was a doctor to clarify his specialty. "Oh," one debutante had said, staking out her claim to marrying-up at a party Quentin knew he never should have attended. "When you said you were a doctor I thought it meant that you *saved* lives."

At least she had been honest, if brutal. He always knew he was too fragile and timid in mental constitution to be a surgeon. Here, alone on the "graveyard" shift, where he had languished for sixteen years, Quentin's only companions were the carloads of bodies belonging to tribes he called the Violently Killed. In a city like New York, such tribes beat their war-drums every night, and even those who thought they shunned such barbarism showed up to the party on Quentin's tables. The Auto Wrecks and the Drunken Accidents and Gang Wars and even the Innocent Bystanders. For too many years their anthropologist, Quentin had catalogued them all.

"I care too," Quent said, wholly to himself.

No one knew.

They would. They would know soon, he kept telling himself; soon, they would know how much.

***

In his pre-med days, Quentin's ability to ace subjects as varied as philosophy, physics, or electrical engineering had been a boon; they impressed admissions committees. Yet his continuing drive to synthesize variant disciplines met with confusion at best. Outside of the particular field in which a term or concept was used, the response to its mention was a blank stare.

With stacks of books and an occasional jerry-rigged device, Quentin worked alone.

He had the time. Why not? He had no other life.

Quentin laughed at himself; why not? The others at the morgue also laughed at him, the kind of silent, unconscious mockery they didn't even perceive, let alone thinking they meant him harm. Consciously, if they thought of him at all they might describe him as shy, and kind. His eunuch-like dedication to his job had found no more release than a half-dozen copies of risqué magazines and couple unusual porno tapes hidden in his closet. Even Quentin's dementias were mild. His asceticism turned him quiet and disheveled in public, made him harmless and asexual in the minds of women he knew. They found him cute. Only when they saw him as impotent was it possible for him to seem attractive.

Quentin stared out over the still air of the morgue. As privileged as many of these still bodies might have been in life, compared to him, they had no such privileged existence now. It was up to him to save their still-living cousins, as they still moved, still breathed and fed and eliminated their wastes, all the while to participate in the *rat-race* and scarcely confront the fact that each would, one day, also become a corpse.

Quentin strode to the examining table. He ran his hand lightly over the sheet, and thus the contours of flesh beneath. The feel of well-formed breasts made him hard. Quentin's back stiffened and he started to pull away, trying to force down the memory of that thrill, and the shame it engendered.

For more than two decades he had been single-minded in his dedication to medical matters. "I've already frittered away so much of my life at this," he had told himself on thousands of nights before, in the same way as this night. "At this point, what's the harm in sacrificing just one evening more?"

He later was unable to remember of an intuitive shock really had coursed through him, filling him with dread even before he yanked back the linen cover and stared at the dead woman's face. The mind was tricky that way; even milliseconds after it thought or felt something, it reconstructed those thoughts and feelings with minor edits. But some things were more certain. The discrepancy between how he would have predicted his actions and feelings—and what really came. The fact he did not cry, or rage, but knew only numbness, and a sudden dropping sensation in his stomach. The dissociated feeling, as if his mind had left his body.

Quentin of all people knew better; knew that that sensation, too, was a lie. But until the shock wore off, he was unable to act.

***

She was his own age. Her expression serene, her soft eyelids closed. The nostrils of her pert nose, sprinkled with freckles, so still. Her hair, golden and sparkling, barely covered the forehead whose ivory skin was so barely marred by a ragged-edged bullet hole. Yet it was neither the sight of her beauty nor her wound that made Quentin's chest tighten and his knees go so numb they started to buckle.

According to the standard conventions determining what constituted "having met" someone, Quentin had never met this dead young woman. Yet he had. Common wisdom also dictated that she was nothing but an object to him, a fantasy image fit for vicarious gratification. Yet to Quentin a few moments of arousal had many times given way to hours of sad pondering.

Who was she, really, when he sought more than a name but an essence? What did she like to eat? Did she like the warmth of a thick blanket under which to curl in a chill room, or would she rather doze on top of the linens, under a tropical moon? In which of these did she find joy? fear? Hope?

Now all those issues needed to be phrased in the past tense.

Then again, she had always existed in the past tense for him, from the first moment he had beheld her in ninth grade chemistry. Years he had carried a secret longing for her, even following her to the local community college when a scholarship to the University of Chicago had been offered to him. Those four years he had avoided her, terrified of facing rejection, perhaps catching a glimpse of her once a month. Until, his libido dampening and the demands of academics mounting, he had started forgetting.

It was a face, a body, that Quentin thought deserved to grace slick magazine photos. And, as attested to by what lay carefully stored in the left-bottom drawer of Quentin's desk at home, her likeness already had seen print. Maybe, Quentin thought, flushing, she was no more than a carved doll to him. Maybe he had never seen her as a person after all. Only the sharp pains between his ribs protested otherwise.

***

The chart read "Jane Doe." Quentin's jaw hardened. None of the names by which he knew her were adequate, yet they were all she had. He saw blue bruises of needle tracks in her arms, and only now noticed the hollow darkness under her eyes, but nothing else marred her skin. Whatever tragedies had befallen her, it seemed they were recent. The bullet wound was the luck of a bad draw, and Quentin had seen the results of enough of those.

He reached out to stroke the flesh he had never before touched, and always wanted to. Now he knew how others felt, pining for a loved one. No matter how much better someone might know a husband or a daughter or a friend, compared to how well Quentin knew her, it was never well enough. This differed from the emotions many might feel upon hearing of his discovery, but only as a variation upon the same theme.

Quentin also felt the desperation they would feel when they lost the first loved one for whom there might be time to be saved.

Six hours. Sweating, Quentin knew too much time had gone by for anything more than an expendable experiment. Gritting his teeth, he knew he had to try to make it more.

***

Quentin's hands moved deftly. He was adept now at working the scalpel through the minimum amount of flesh and muscle. Then came the placement of thin needles, both on her skin and through the hairline incisions.

The patterns in which he moved were particular, and left no room for error. Though in concept not unlike the Eastern principles of *hara*, or *chakra*, or *chi*, such primitive conceptions were more a liability than a guide. One needed the correct stimulation of the whole organism, but only in the proper sequence of stimulation of the parts. Nor could a surface approach suffice; penetrating the skin to stimulate deep muscle and nerve and organs was even more vital than the skin-level stimulation.

Quentin glanced at his stopwatch. She had been dead for eight hours now. Time was running out. Already, invisible to the naked eye, at the cellular level, tissue was degrading. Unregulated enzymes, no longer participating in a closed and communal chemical loop, selfishly chewed each cell's important organelles. It was already too late to resuscitate her permanently; that opportunity had passed mere minutes after her original demise. But he could give her back a few, brief moments, as impoverished as her thought-processes would be.

He shook his head violently, trying to dispel the mounting headache. It never bothered him before that this was an experiment, that even if it seemed useless there was value, data to contribute to refinements in procedure that would make future procedures more than short-term. Clinically applicable.

Quentin quickly donned the jerry-rigged wetsuit, in whose rubber was embedded an array of sensors. The patterns in which her both her body and all its parts needed stimulation were impossibly complex to simply store and run off a digital computer, even were it done on the state-of-the-art supercomputers. Realizing this truth, accepting it, had led directly to his breakthrough of using a living creature's own metabolism as a crude template.

Pneuma, the ancient Greeks had called the stuff of soul, using the same word as "breath." This *pneuma* was made of no matter in particular but an incompressible pattern; this *pneuma* was what they shared.

Needle electrodes against her nerves now stimulated tremors in corresponding muscle. The patterns would bear fruit if the process were painstakingly followed in all its length and tedium. Quentin let the current flow, examining him, and then flowing into her, phased in certain peculiar, non-repeating sequences. Finally, as was necessary, the dynamics of the field began to exceed properties that could be explained by mere classical electromagnetic theory.

Quentin lost track of time; of course, when Time was a physical property whose characteristics changed subtly in a quantum-coherent field, and they both now bathed in one. He forced himself out of the trance and looked at the clock. The night shift would be over in two hours. If she awoke now, they would have just enough time together to see if it worked.

Quentin disconnected himself from the apparatus and stepped back.

The five or more minutes necessary for the cumulative effect dragged, for him, into an eternity. Then, jerking, haltingly, her hand moved.

It was a slim, smooth hand, once tan but now overlaid with a white hue, like chalk dust. She lifted the linen. Then she sat up and stood before him. Naked as Eve.

For a moment, she seemed to comprehend. Her gaze focused on him and her round lips, still red from the lipstick she had been wearing when shot, formed a puckering circle. Quentin's heart thudded painfully against his ribs, not knowing whether to hope she would speak. For months he had sought to perform a resurrection where the subject was obviously aware, and could say so. But this was not a mere test subject, it was *her*, and it was a near-certainty that he had raised her from the dead for only a few moments. The sensation was the same as over the course of countless long-past afternoons, when Quentin had not known whether to hope for a chance at her attention or dread it.

Then, just as all the others' eyes had, hers turned dull. Quentin held out his hand. She took it, much too obediently.

***

Quentin's head swam. An hour left. An hour, which would pass with agonizing slowness if he terminated the experiment now, as he had all the others. He had marched her around the room, gotten her to sit and stand, to turn her head and grasp objects, yet each act was in a stereotyped motion that gave Quentin no indication she was thinking independently in anything more than a minimal way. And a minimal way was not enough.

Not enough. Not when the promise of resurrection he could hand to the world came as all such elixirs did: with a price.

Some theorists had long since hypothesized that quantum events in the weird, seemingly mystical subatomic realm were necessary to explain Life, or Consciousness. These theorists had potent critics who pointed out that the physiochemical dynamics of cells and organs and brains, despite being microscopic, were still too large for quantum effects to matter.

The problem was, both camps were wrong. And that also meant, in ways to which they were blind, each camp was partially *right.*

"It's like a bridge," Quentin said, looking away himself. "Say the most of it has to be constructed of wood, because stone will collapse under its own weight. But say the footings still have to be made of stone. The stone is like the quantum effects— their proportion of the bridge is small, even if the bridge's footings are necessary. Meanwhile, standard physiology, with its non-linear dynamics, runs the vast majority of the show. It's a classic, non-symmetric, imbalanced synergism."

Quentin turned back to her. She pawed lightly at her suit, ineffectually.

Quent shook his head. What use was it, to go on talking? He could tell her the quantum proponents always had looked for too large a phenomenon, for quantum effects that could be seen across a whole cell, or even groups of cells. Experiments didn't find any, of course; because they expected too much.

So no one but him ever would have pondered whether large scale quantum effects that didn't exist presently could be amplified when the non-linear dynamics part of the synergy was failing, with an *externally* sourced quantum coherence that *did* bridge entire groups of cells before too much tissue became necrotic.

A miracle. But, in the end, still a physical phenomenon.

The vast majority of humanity believed in a "soul," clamored for proof of it, and stubbornly disregarded proof against it. "Well, I found it," Quentin mumbled. "The problem is, it's mortal. Just like a body, it gets messed up. Just like a body, when it's messed up badly enough, it dies."

He stroked her cold cheek and added, "Dies, and never comes back."

What would the people of the world say, facing verification that there was no definite afterlife and that all the lives lost in history had slipped into Void? Would people welcome the opportunity to live forever, in the company of loved ones already alive and maintained by science, if it meant confronting the truth that those dead and buried were truly no more? Would they adore Quentin, this new prophet? Or seethe with contempt at this heretic, this blasphemer who robbed them of their cherished beliefs?

"Could they accept me," Quentin asked her, "when I'm even finding it difficult, when I see you again, when having you here doesn't mean jack when I just have to part with you, again, still never knowing you this time either?"

He thought she shrugged, but meaningless spasms were something he'd seen with earlier subjects.

Quentin doubted he ever had possessed the willpower to fight the multitudes who would oppose this. The religious who science as Evil, atheist, yet picked-and-chose like they did with all science, using the technology without confronting the challenges to their own beliefs. New Age flakes who loved quantum phenomena only because they thought it supported magick, astrology, or bizarre quasi-Eastern mysticism. Academic philosophers and logicians who had built ivory towers on classical logic, algorithms, Mind as "no more than a computer," and stubbornly insisted quantum effects were no place to look.

None of them saw their fundamental similarities. All sought an *essence* to life, something removable from that of which it was made.

"Flesh," Quentin said.

The woman he had wanted to love so much, one who in another life he even might have been fortunate enough to love, ignored him. All she did was walk in a dull, stereotyped shuffle back-and-forth across a too-clean floor.

"Say my name," he implored her. "Say, Q.E.D."

***

Not knowing what she was doing, at least as far as Quentin could tell, she came to him. She walked to the cold, shiny examination table upon which Quentin sat, and she stood at his side as if at perfect military attention.

Choking back tears, Quentin looked away. But he could not resist, after a few moments, looking back. Her dilated pupils stared at him and she leaned her head toward him, tipping it quizzically. Compelled, Quentin reached up to touch her cheek. It was still clammy, though a bit warmer than the sixty degrees of the laboratory. Without a quick enough resurrection procedure, her body was incapable of generating much of its own heat.

Still exploring and confused as a child, she did what he had dreamed of for countless summers, and touched her lips to his. They were cold.

Weeping freely now, Quentin stood and took her in his arms. They danced. No tune played, but then the sounds of music would only confound her. She simply matched his own motion, and he made sure to move slowly enough. As though moving in water they slowly whirled and glided and dipped.

Quentin took her slim neck and pushed her lips to his. She barely responded, but did not pull away. He probed her mouth with his tongue, lacking in practice and operating on a decade-old memory. She tried to emulate him with even less success, twining her fingers in his hair and working her mouth fish-like, mechanical.

Quentin cupped a breast in his hand; it was too firm, almost like rigor mortis, though that was impossible in adipose tissue, and Quentin had to be careful not to disrupt the delicate electrode needles emanating like porcupine quills from various parts of her body. Her nipples, of course stiff, were chill to his tongued kisses.

Quentin forced his hands to make circles over the firmness of her stomach, the indention of her navel, the soft hair between her thighs. He moved in-between them, his cock painfully hard. Yet he could never enter her, could not remove the sensor-imbedded wetsuit without her dying, as much as she struggled to tighten her legs around him as if desperate for the feeling.

***

Quentin led the pale form back to her table. She followed, still obedient.

He stroked her hair ever so gently as he delayed the lethal injection of tetrodotoxin he used to end each experiment a little prematurely, and make sure the subject didn't die in pain. Even with the aid of Quentin's resurrection techniques, her vitality began to ebb, and she laid down.

What was the use? Quentin thought as he twirled the now-hated syringe between his fingers. What was the use? Even with the aid of his techniques death could not be forestalled forever. A horrendous accident could always disrupt a body's matter beyond the hope of even an advanced resuscitation setup. All Quentin had done was prolong life, and with it intensified the disappointment at its end.

What was the use? Quentin thought as he watched her eyes cloud over, now certain that these few brief moments he had given her were irrelevant at best, or a curse at worst.

Not bothering to remove the wetsuit, Quentin reversed the syringe and plunged it into his own heart.

He never felt the grasp on his shoulder of a hand, fighting from beneath a shroud, trying to stop him.

He never heard her weeping voice, nearly incapable of speech but grateful for one more moment to feel and think and try, struggle to beg him, "No."

BIOS (Basic Input Output System) v.1.1

Given Robert Subiaga, Jr.'s undergraduate education in neurophysiology, his graduate education in philosophy, his endless obsession with the mind-body problem, and his seven year stint doing research, you might be tempted to believe parts of the short story published in this issue are based on real events.

Nothing could be further from the truth.

Subiaga, for example, never has had sex with any real corpses. Only Lutherans.

H.E.L.L.

Heaven died
    one dark night.
Eves when Angels
    forgot to tread
Lanes on which whose
    travelers, if dead
Lacked not the grace
    of harsh insight

(1982)

6367828

Who calls among the dead?

(calls to me?)

Here, among the fallen

I lie

  in state, unmourned

My soul the one

  dead,

  body spared.

Nothing

but a shell, to mock

the very idea of

  Existence.

(1982)

EXCALIBUR

Who took that ore

from the mothering earth?

Whose divine hand

plunged it into the fire

 and bellowed the forge hot?

Smelted and fired

by the blue flame

of passion?

Tempered by

the cold touch

of snowy hells?

Ground, as teeth, by anger

to a diamond edge?

Steel, that holds no warmth.

Until a sword, of unparalleled

excellence, that must now be

shut away.

Or will be

blooded.

(1982)

THE LYRE

Come, balladeer, sing me of Beauty—

then taste the blood of my wounded lyre.

What know you of these mutant shapes

lurking' bout our waiting pyre?

Underworld winds tremble all Earths,

But will your tales speak to blackest the Rose?

Or do fires do quiver, in their own hearths,

and pale Balder find no succor, in prose?

Perhaps pharaohs wonder, long in their tombs

at inexorable Fates no Sphinx even knows;

Answers still sought, since the days of the womb—

and still lost every Age as it draws to close.

Last battles draw nearer, with every day,

with each other the Serpent now girds his whole
length;

yet you'll kneel to a Heaven that's never held
sway:

empty myths, devoid of sinew or strength.

Quiet Solomon lies in his glory, lies still

but the All persists, while even all fall;

and someone's hands will devour and swill

even after we haunt Death's long, empty hall.

So call on your gods—no verses they'll hear,

Nor do your Angels ever answer such cries.

But Life alone lives, the Passion that Kills:

our true mate, the Goddess, crimson Her eyes.

(1982)

DIALOGOS

Omne ignotum pro magnifico est.

Sit ut est aut non sit.

"You have passed the test. You have been chosen."

The stranger with only one good eye looked up at her in response to her words. His expression was quizzical, not extending as far toward suppressed fear as she was accustomed to receiving in her presence. But he did show he caught the strangeness in her melodic voice.

Her speech was almost like a song, echoing near-imperceptibly in her own throat and forming an inhuman resonance. Her speech was almost like a song, and as hypnotic.

She knew what he would see, looking at her, though it was true she never had beheld her own countenance. Her long hair, of brilliant black sheen; her slim, pale-skinned limbs, as smooth as ivory; her narrow waist and full hips and small, firm breasts. And the shimmering depths of her eyes, whose color even she could not know, did not know.

His arousal and appreciation were inevitable, she knew. The helplessness of her chosen ones always was. Thus, that must be why this one repressed too clear a show of the creeping terror he must needs experienced.

The stranger was a mercenary from somewhere west of these Polish borderlands. His left eye was covered by a brown leather patch that bore intricate embroidery, perhaps of some long unused rune. Likely the eye's dysfunction was caused by some wound, as she saw a scar on both his eyebrow above, and the upper part of his cheek below, no doubt the scar stretching in-between. His other eye, its iris a dull grey like the metal of an oft-used blade, fixed itself on her.

"It is time for the tavern to close," she said.

"Not to guests of the inn upstairs," he replied. "You are welcome to accompany me to my room."

"That is not where I rest," she said. "No. I will settle for nothing less than my domain. The other men have sat here tonight, chatted idly, each hoping he would be allowed to accompany me home. But like a master at chess or draughts, you made all the right moves."

"I passed the test," he reminded her of her words sardonically.

"You have been chosen," she corrected.

"You are open with your opinion," he noted.

"I am open with my truth," she said. "And I know men. I know their hearts."

" When one is attractive one hears all the approaches of suitors."

"Aye. And I am not only fair, of both countenance and choice, but merciless."

"Should that boast cause me trepidation?" he said.

"I will drain you. Leave a husk. And you will not care."

"Well, then," he said, rising and reaching for his cloak. "If I am so compelled, we may as well go."

***

They moved to the door. The mercenary's large frame was covered in woolens and leather, and he donned a long leather riding coat whose hem reached nearly to the floor, such as some wore in the *ukrainia*, these borderlands, and called themselves *kozaki*. Mostly Tatar, they also had a rich collection of thieves, outlaws, and simply Slav frontiersman who wished to live clear of the rivalries between Poland, the Turks, the Mongols, and Muscovy.

The mercenary's skin was the color of bronze, but his features and long, straight, jet-black hair, braided at his temples, showed him neither Turk, nor Tatar either. Nor was his sword, a long, straight, two handed broadsword he now slung unscabbarded across his back, common in these regions. The long, braided-leather whip and *kozak*-style long knife at his belt, however, were weapons familiar to this region.

"What could I receive, by coming to your bed, that would interest me?" he said, not hiding his interest as he held the door for her and they braved the wind-shipped snow. Not hiding his interest, but still showing more restraint than she had ever before encountered.

"Great Pleasure," she said, more intrigued. "Great delight. You will lose yourself, your sense of *self*, until you do not care what more I might do with you. When you will beg for what more I might do, though you have no more to give."

"I see."

"No. You do not. But come."

"The hour is late and the wine-barrels tend toward empty," he admitted.

"Empty grows the source of the courage, and the solace, that men find here."

"Men, such as your prior lovers."

"Men, such as I devoured."

"Men, such as were chosen." He gave a wry, closed-mouthed smile. "My own coat may be insufficient, if we walk the winter night; I would express regard for the inadequacy of your dress, but if your spirit is as ravenous as you say my concern should be unwarranted."

She felt anger tighten her, then sighed and replied, "The wine you have drunk and your ardor will keep you warm."

"For as long as you let me keep it, I suppose."

***

They soon reached the edge of town and continued onward. "I will ask you to retain humility and discretion in your thoughts," she said to him, "for we are not to the place of the Taking yet, and what you fantasize of is premature."

"And of what do I think?" he asked. "Do you read my mind?"

"Your thoughts are as visible to me as an opened book. I, instead, am a tome of ancient riddles, nested verses, unending questions."

"Of course."

"Do not mock me."

"And will showing you deference avert my Fate?"

She started. So simple a question had not come to the minds of any of her other chosen ones. Why, indeed, should he bow a knee, when in the End it made no difference?

The hour grew late. Her hunger the greater. As if she were in actuality the one buffeted by powers beyond her control.

"Do not mock me," she repeated, her voice cracking. "Your past, your memories are a door soon to be shut; your future a fathomless void. But I can give you the last adventure of a dying passion, linking them in one last burst, looming as something to anticipate."

"Your magic will quake my world," he said. "As it makes it grow still." He sighed. "The Franks do call orgasm 'the little death.'"

"Yours will in no way be so small," she said.

"And you will kill me at the zenith of the darkness. Or is it at the height of ecstasy?"

"I know not, for when I am done no one has risen to say."

"And there is no chance I would survive."

"I assure you, no."

***

"Are we far?"

"It is difficult to tell. The distance we travel is not a line."

"Not straight," he said. "Yet perhaps even all curves are but an infinity of infinitesimally small lines."

"You wallow in the rules of man, that would split hairs of logic, mathematics, science – bereft of power in the realm of my world, of dark and primal magicks."

"I assure you," the mercenary mirrored her earlier words back at her, giving her another start, "no."

***

"The night is a fit path for us to walk," she said. "The darkness is my home. I am at peace. Yet in that peace I hunger, and ache for the Taking."

"Well and well," he said. "Do you propose to overpower me, when I am so much larger than you?"

"Larger, but not stronger. Yours is the strength of two average men, perhaps three; but I have that of at least twenty of them."

"If not twenty of me," he told her.

"More, it is the strength that cannot be quantified, only qualified," she said, trying to ignore his prosaic attitude. "That of all the dark places, of caves, of pits, of cairns and graves, of the depths of moist earth. Heaped mounds of burial, and timeless secrets. Ages of practices nearly forgotten, but never lost to me."

"And I am but a prize to you," he said. "Part of a game, one you play as if to win even as you never even wished to play."

"You skirt the perimeters of honesty," she replied. "More, the truth is: you do not know how to deal with me."

"I do, and I do not. Such is the way of all things."

"Do not deny your own arousal, little man! The means by which you will be put to rest. Not the sleep that is natural after the exhaustion of passions, but the one most sound, aye; and lasting until the Final Trumpet. Our destination?" Her full, red lips stretching to a smile. "Here. Just to one side of the path."

"The graveyard."

"That lies to our right, but I do not dwell on the right. Not in the eyes of Man's morality, nor to the right hand of any of his 'Gods.' You see your hallowed ground; I sleep to the left. You think me monster, yet the hunger that cannot be sated, no one can I touch without his being consumed, no heart shared save his weaker one devoured, was not what I chose, but was forced on me."

"Then we are all such monsters," he said.

"None such as I!"

"Self-pity. Such a common indulgence."

"While you partake of your demise freely," she sneered.

"Indeed. Your spell has worked. I am entranced."

"So wild!" she began to stretch and languidly ripple like a slim and pale panther in a thin white dress. "So still. As it always was. Will you dare kiss me in the shadow of Life's Tree, where as I do a hawk nests in the branches, and you are the mouse, prey to my power of silent flight? Am I crazed? When such as you are lost in the blink of my eye while I have been caressed by Egyptian winds, my lips curried by the eunuchs of Cathay's court? Am I not what you desired, deep in your heart? Leave you will? Can you?"

He sighed wearily. Cocked an eyebrow. "Now that you mention it," he said, turning, matter-of-factly, "Yes." And back to her, began to walk away.

***

She had been through the Taking how many times
before? A hundred? A thousand? More? Each had
been a unique creature, frail and full of potential,
and warmth. Each a full-blooded human being; yet
in the end, each a drained husk of quivering flesh,
on its quick way to dust.

Yet none before such as this, to make her eyes
burn with not only the passions of lust, but also of
rage. How dare he? *How dare he?*

Still, as countless times before, her preternatural
strength moved faster than any eye could follow,
catching up with him and bending the mercenary
back sharply until it almost seemed his back would
break. I spoke fact, her thoughts hissed, striking
out in the direction of his mind with such speed
that the space between seconds could hold her
soliloquy. Draw me close – look into my deep
wells of silence; see how silver they are? The fire
is cold, the fire is need. Around us snow is deep
and even – I touch this dark limb and snowflakes
cascade down. Like the seconds remaining in your
life. Silent, swallowed by the drifts of time that
melt in the sun of existence. You will not scream.
One cannot in dreams; and soon your sleep will be
most sound, and even dreamless. As I embrace
you, look back at the ground we've covered. Only

50

one set of footprints exists there. One unsteady track on crystals of frost and stainless snow. Here they will find you. But I shall be gone, ancient and cold, leaving no tracks but your own, in your attempt to walk with me. And tell me: am I not *Truth*?

And then, without realizing how such a thing could be, she was hurtling through the air, in a flight she had not caused, and was unable to stop.

***

The motion, as disorienting as it was, seemed slowed to her senses; though less, now, for the fact she was inhumanly fast than that she had *lost control.*

She caught a glimpse behind her of the mercenary, unbalanced but not quite falling, his booted left leg extended and cupped. The leg that had swept her own out from under her as, rather than resist her attack, he had rolled along with it and even added momentum of his own falling body.

Momentum all focused in a direction *he* had dictated and *she*, not expecting, had been unable to resist.

For the briefest fraction of a second as she hurtled through the air she felt a hot surge of anger. Then first her shoulder, then her head, and finally the rest of her body touched earth.

The earth of the cemetery. Consecrated earth.

The pain was immediate. The realization she was burning a fraction of a second later.

Immediately she leapt to her feet, smoke billowing off her, struggling to climb back over the fence and out of the cemetery. As she was halfway over the wooden rail her head was suddenly jerked backward as she heard a thin crack and felt the bite of a whip wrap around her neck.

The mercenary's strength alone, at the other end of the whip, was dwarfed by her strength; but with such a high fulcrum and all her force generated by her legs, far lower, the leverage was his.

Unbalanced on top of the fence, no support against which to brace herself, her own power caused to her flip. She fell back onto the cemetery ground once more.

She rose and faced her the mercenary this time. Her grimaced fangs exuded a reverberating growl, her eyes now glowed crimson, and she rushed him. But her attack was reckless, a combination of much anger and even more panic, to which she was unaccustomed. This time the mercenary whirled and dropped into a split-legged stance, his thick arms grasping her firmly and sending her hurtling over his hips.

Her strength was already waning from being trapped on sanctified ground, and this time when she dropped to it she felt an unfamiliar sensation: the shattering of three ribs.

Her long arms went from lithe to gaunt as the burning skin along them started to desiccate. Clawing, scrabbling along the frozen ground, both burning and somehow numbed by an icy cold to which she had just moments before been immune, she struggled for the fence that had only gotten father away.

The mercenary's silhouette seemed to hover over her.

She rolled over on her back and tried in vain to reach up toward it, to claw it with the same long, razor-sharp fingernails that had ripped countless victims from crotch to clavicle in the past, to expose a still-warm heart she would consume.

Her flailing hands came up short. The point of the mercenary's claymore broadsword smashed through her breastbone and pinned her to this killing ground.

Clotting blood bubbled up her throat as she tried to speak, the down-sloping arms of the claymore's guard working with handle and blade to form an unusual cross as limned against the purple, moonless sky.

"You are no mere warrior," she accused, " ... but a wizard ..."

"And you, *rusalka*?" he gave a sad chuckle, and a sigh. "What are you? You take your deficiencies and call it proof your abilities cannot be defined or contained," he said, kneeling over her. "Allege hidden wells of power, then when opposed by raw strength, you decry power as crass. Assert yours is a primal force that cannot be matched, yet keen that you are oppressed." He leaned on the sword. "'Truth?'" he said, almost sadly. "Perhaps."

"You lie ...," she spat her last bloody breath at him.

Her final image of him looking to the cold moon setting on the blacker hills. And saying, "I merely am."

THE CAVALIER

The Cavalier, he rode the road,

cavalier his mood

when across the path, came disheveled maid

and broke the interlude

Haggard of hair, and haggard of gown

she stumbled before his mount,

and though she spoke not a thing at first

her state of need was paramount

"How came you now, to this state,"

he asked the black-eyed Miss,

but she only lifted pale face to his

and locked him in a kiss.

Behind those eyelids, he'd let slip closed

in passion, but cold heat

a billion visions flooded in

and now slowed his heartbeat

Countless children, he saw born,

countless, he saw die

each passing trade, for another life

each smile bought by wet eyes.

Joys and pain, in twain linked,

as Shadows and the Light

and both, then, each others' cloaks,

suffused in Day and Night

She pulled away, and now her gaze

was not blank, but full of fright;

he whispered, "what ask you, of me now,"

his knowing chest drawn tight.

Here was the herald, of the Void;

the Reaper, come to this side;

Sin-eater, doomed to her role,

from whom all would flee and hide.

But not, to gather him She came

this was not yet his time;

but with pleading face, merely asked,

he take her place, in line.

Rejected, feared, and despised,

she walked this Earth alone.

Unless a willing one be found,

to allow her to go home.

In-between, did she walk

belonging to no one world;

be it flesh and spirit, life or death,

no single flag unfurled.

I have love for all, Her eyes did say,

but none can full know Me.

And still must choose, choose or not,

who shall know tragedy.

Share relieved triumph, of the foe

even as the vanquished's tears;

know the joys, of beating life,

who feeds on stilled hearts' fears.

Will this burden, you relieve,

she asked, with trembling hands

in his, and implored, that she might rest

and in her place he stand.

But with frightened chest, shaking hard,

he found there was a place

that abject fear could grip his breast

and make him turn his face.

Suddenly, with sunken cheeks,

and a grimace tinged of hate,

She said: I've erred, no champion's here,

who'd save Me from my Fate.

Just a would-be saint, who'd but keep

reputation free of stain,

as on my hands, red stands the blood,

and on my heart the pain.

Then cavalier, as comes to all,

Reap indeed I will,

and in the morning, did those on the path,

come upon him, still.

His staring eyes, only marked,

by a single, trickling tear,

that he'd true failed, that maid in need

for a pristine image, dear.

(1984)

PEACE

Peace is a rainbow, colored

shades of all rust.

Peace is a rose, hiding

blooded thorns, in good trust.

Peace is Death's beloved,

Only-begotten Son.

But you are right, my dear,

I have no fear: by way

of Peace, shall we all

one day

be One.

(1984)

THE ELDEST EDDA

The moon was cold and clear;

wind-blown sand crossed the lea.

But a tavern on a cliff fell silent,

as doors opened to the sea.

With the chills, there crept in fear;

and mulled wine lost its glee.

For, framed 'gainst the stars, there stood a Man

and much more, in same body.

The patrons eyed him fearfully

but ne'er a word was spoke.

It was the shaking tavern-keeper

who, the tableau broke.

"Old friend, what do you now and near,

whom we had long thought dead?

How good it is to see you here;

come, share our Salt, and Bread."

The Man's eyes laughed, as Tigers laugh

when filled with killing lust:

a sword whose naked, sharpened shine

ne'er—and always—be tinted rust.

And unbidden, His hidden memories

broke out and shared their flesh.

To form the last tale of He who they

had only, long, thought dust.

Unknown, somewhere, a Battle had raged

until all armies' fall.

With no hand left, on either side,

to raise a rally call.

But as the Man lay, His thick blood

irrigating muddy ground,

within His ears, did Heaven's trumpets

blow with Hell's own sound.

The warrior Man was lifted up;

placed on new horse, to ride.

And travelling, did now He find

The Devil at His side.

"Old Friend," did proud Devil say,

"I see your End grows nigh.

But ride with me, pillage with me;

Reign again ... just as second-Most High!"

The Man said nothing, and soon found

even the Devil could He burn.

That, for such generous offers,

one might yet stay taciturn.

"Come, my friend," the Devil did say,

don't, to me, play profound!

Look to those you have been bane;

the blood *you've* fed the ground!

"You belong to me," did Devil now say,

"It appears in every Sign.

Nor does it do, to fight your End

when in it, all men are mine."

The Man drew His sword, whispered harsh,

"I'll not submit to a darkness so … small.

"Still, all you need do is take me,"

snarled a Man, free after all.

Tale done, black ale finished,

He placed His Cup back down.

Without a word, out door He strode,

what more, without a sound.

Not again did any there see the Eye,

His one good eye's ice-stare.

That ever, with His ravens rides

—even if Valhalla lies bare.

(1984)

ONCE AN EAGLE

Once an eagle, broken of wing

born a fledgling, looking down

from heights where pebbles fall

like dreams.

Once an eagle, who

too much knows, the bird

with broken pinion

never flies so high

again.

Once an eagle, broken-winged

tried and spread and soared

if for an instant only

frozen.

Evermore.

(1984)

WOLVES TALES, 1

This is a story that happened long ago. But not so long that it is forgotten—or one should not take seriously.

It happened in what you, dear listener, often call the North Woods, in the era where French men called Voyageurs were making their first forays up the rivers and into the forests in search of pelts and furs. Though most of these white men were peripatetic as fit their profession, and there were not even many of them yet, following their trails came an aging man from what is now Germany, seeking a private new life far from where he had grown up.

He built himself a cabin, set apart mostly from either the seasonal camps of the Voyageurs or the native tribes, but able to venture when needed to either for very occasional trade. And there, alone, he lived for many more years, subsisting and even, for a single man, prospering as he lived off the land.

Eventually, however, the solitude he had sought turned to a crushing loneliness. It may not have, you might suspect, had he not somehow become the target of correspondence from the old country. But, in any case, he became a participant in an exchange with a beautiful, much younger woman from near his childhood town, and she lamented that she too was both lonely, but somehow at the same time pined for a life like his. A life with only one or a few loved ones true, but otherwise in the beauty and solitude of the woods.

Finally, the old man wrote a last letter saying that he would marry her, if, somehow, she could abide being the wife of someone such as he, and she accepted, and came across the sea on a long journey and became his wife.

Soon she was pregnant, and bore him a baby boy. And for the first time in his life, the old man knew not merely contentment, but happiness.

As months passed after the birth of their son, however, a shadow came over the old man's new joy. For on one of his rare occasions to visit and trade with the Voyageurs who had brought his bride up the rivers to him, the old man found that his best friend among them was missing and presumed dead. In fact, one or two such traders had disappeared each of the previous few months. Scarcely was there ever found a trace of the missing man as well; at most a streak dragged through pines needles, or perhaps a few drops of blood here or there.

The stealth and expertise with which each missing man had been abducted, sometimes mere yards from his comrades as they slept or ate and drank around the fire, greatly disturbed the Voyageurs. Some whispered of monstrous creatures of the night. But others started grumbling that it could only be the result of attacks from the nearby tribe, though they had had only sporadic contact and at that excellent relations for nearly two decades.

The simple solution might have been to send an envoy to talk to the tribe, but resentment and anger had been kindled so fast in the wake of the disappearances that the old man feared any contact broaching the subject would open with bitterness, and maybe even quick violence.

Concerned, and having a close friendship with the elder among the tribe most responsible for advising his people on matters of medicine, the old man went straight on the two day trek from the

Voyageur camp to the current village. There, the old man was received by his old friend the elder, and they supped. But the elder seemed muted in his expressions of happiness that the old man had found his bride and love, and a darkness came over the elder as the old man described now being a father.

As impolite as it was, the old man pressed the subject. The elder, along with his concern, expressed a confusion as well. "Your ways are not always the same as ours," the elder said, "nor your spirits, or gods, or demons. There is much I do not know about the burden I can sense you carry. But your bloodline bears a curse I cannot identify, from the land of your birth."

The old man pleaded for anything more the elder could tell him, but the elder only gave a wan smile and told him, uncertainly, that he caught glimpses of the spirit of a Wolf, but not as a guide and not naturally. It even reminded him of what he knew of as a *wendigo*, whose heart was made of ice and whose appetite cannot be satisfied.

"I know nothing of its like among my people, or my lands," the elder told him, "nor have I seen or heard of its exact like." But then the elder pointed to the old man's silver wedding band and said, "though I do know, somehow, that that is a substance it fears."

The old man thanked his friend and left, returning to his cabin. But when he returned, though it was so late as to nearly be the start of false dawn, when he came back to the cabin he found it empty and his infant son alone near the well-stocked hearth fire.

When dawn had almost broken, the old man, who had been dozing, awakened to his young wife returning from the woods, laden with two buckets. She told her husband she had to go to the stream for water, and to the storehouse for food for the boy, who was just starting to wean.

The next month, the full moon came before the old man noticed, and once more on its first night he woke in the middle of the darkness to find his wife gone. He waited for her return, and again it was not for many hours. The next day, his heart sinking, the old man ventured to the new Voyageur camp, which was not so far away this time, fearing that he would find that another man or two had gone missing.

This time, no such thing was the case. But it was far worse.

No one had disappeared without any trace, but there were no bodies either. Just torn tents, tatters of flesh and copious blood smears, and drag marks through the trees and over the trails giving clear indication that everyone was dead. Amid the blood and gore, the unmistakable odor of musket fire that, nevertheless, had somehow been ineffectual.

Heart pounding, the old man returned to the cabin and nervously told his wife he would be gone for a few days to visit the native village again. Moving as quickly as he could, the old man traversed the distance to see his friend the elder. But as he came into view of the village, the old man was greeted with a similar scene as he had seen at the Voyageur camp. Everyone here, too, was dead.

When the old man came across the body of his friend the elder, his heart sank even further. Clutched in the elder's hand was a pewter trade goblet he apparently had tried to use as a weapon, in desperation, the closest thing to the silver he had pointed out on the old man's wedding ring. Not that it had been wholly ineffectual—for in those days pewter sometimes still bore traces of silver with the tin, as this one did—and there was a bit of dark blood and a tuft of fur clinging to the rim of the goblet.

Rushing back home, the old man came to his cabin in the dead of night again—and again, his young wife was gone, though the baby was safe in his bascinet and the fire well stoked.

Trembling, the old man felt he knew what he had to do. He took his bullet mold, in the heat of the blazing hearth melted his wedding band, and cast a single shot of pure silver for his large bore pistol. His heart tearing in his chest he loaded the single round ball and the largest amount of powder the pistol could bear without rupturing—or perhaps large enough to rupture, as if hoping that should he use it he might fatally injure himself as well.

Once again, it was many hours before the young wife returned. The old man was dozing in the large chair he had set before the cabin door when it started to creak open. And with only her silhouette against the moon, he raised the pistol as if still in a half-dream, and fired a shot through her heart. The barrel of the pistol did indeed burst at the same time, though only enough to send fragments of powder into his eyes and partially blind him, and when his beloved fell over the threshold and he ran to her, his eyes would have been streaming with tears anyway.

Though his vision was blurred, he looked into her shocked gaze and she died, unable to escape the look of wonderment and confusion on her face. Weeping, the old man knew nothing but how, as for the rest of his life, other than his son, he would know nothing but crushing loneliness again.

But, perhaps mercifully, a loneliness that would not last long.

As behind him, the old man heard the bascinet creak and groan, as if something suddenly too massive to be contained by it was coming out, and toward him. Something from his bloodline. His, not hers.

And the last thing he heard was the growl, of a wolf, but one whose hunger that could never be fully satisfied. A last sound for him to hear, under the light of the moon.

EX CATHEDRA

Through the blizzard,
perched in the tree in wait
armed to kill. Gazing
at the evergreen spires on hillsides.
Hillside, upon hillside. All bearing
snow, heavy, as pagan giants' limbs.
Any movement is stillborn;
other than only the fluttering
of flakes, coming down
through the storm.
No prey in sight.
The cutaway up the ridge
opens up doors
of an emerald cathedral;
I hide upon a spire and wait,
looking up, looking down.
Any cardinals in hiding;
as are the bishops.
But red squirrels take shelter,
and mockingly throw
incense from the pines.
When I descend, the wind at my back
seems to push me, more than I walk

under my own power,
past those once-spires,
now tangled and cracked, fallen
into the narrow paths.
Snow muffling every step.
But I stop every few,

and look back.

Lot's wife be damned.
There is no harm, if only
every once in a while,
in looking back.

(1986)

WINDOWSILLS

On how many

windowsills

do old skins still

wait, for new wine:

functional spirits,

ready to be

used, but unused

to the searing

of lips?

(1986)

SHE

The *rusalka* had

another name

that smothered

my face, full lips

embraced mine, or so,

feeling like

I was

floating, but

in reality

underwater,

I dreamt. Once.

(1986)

COUNTING THE SECONDS, SINCE THE LIGHTNING

(a pseudo-haiku)

Charged grey air

another autumn

a feeling I thought

would save me.

Dying.

(1986)

THE SHREW THAT ATE RUSH LIMBAUGH

Han stopped writing on the blackboard and turned to the students, his deep-set eyes searching from behind his glasses. Eyes that could see through their skin and muscle and blood.

Han also saw through the electrochemical spiking of their nerve cell impulses, made meager by the lights and whirrs and beeps of video games and sitcoms. Into the convoluted tubes of their kidneys' glomeruli, which strained to filter all the by-products of Doritos and Big Macs and 3.2-percent Shinkelbaker beer, the cheapest on the market and easily available in convenience stores that always seemed to "forget" the check ID's. *My genius, a real Second Sight, watches the careening path of hormones in their circulation, linking their overactive groins to their undisciplined brains and*

...

"Mr. Davies?"

"Huh?" Han said, the thoughts of his rarefied mind suddenly ricocheting too much to form coherent words. Had he been standing still for too long a time without saying or writing anything?

"Oh. Yes, I'm sorry. Where was I, Carrie?" *And why don't you shut up, you snot-nosed brat?*

Han wiped a trembling hand across his brow. There were still fifteen minutes to go in the period; why couldn't the class just leave him alone? Why did he even try? Indeed, communicating what the brightest of them could comprehend was still but slumming to him. He'd only taken up teaching to pay the bills when those bastards at UIT wouldn't recognize his genius and grant him more than a masters' degree, insisting their Ph.D.'s were for "the people who ask the Big Questions." *A science prodigy as a kid and instead of an upper-level executive position at some high-technology bioengineering firm I'm here, baby-sitting for twenty-grand a year ...*

Wishing they would leave him alone. Knowing that couldn't happen. Not while his genius, the equivalent of a Second Sight, let him keep seeing right through them.

"Mr. Davies? You were saying something about proportions?"

Proportions. "Ah, yes. Proportions are the key to the Laws of Physics. When one value changes all the others in the equation must also change. A spider, for example, could never be the house-sized killer of grade-B horror films. Can anyone tell me why?"

Lamar raised his hand, but did not wait to be called on before blurting his answer. "The Square-Cube Rule," he said.

"Explain further," Han said, unimpressed.

"Well ...," Lamar started. "It's ... it's like ...," he struggled to say, looking about himself for help from his classmates. Han shot them all a disapproving look, however, as if to threaten them into leaving Lamar to sink or swim of his own accord.

All but one obeyed. "Certain physical properties like mass and volume are results of a length taken to the third power, or cubed," Warren Zyba said prosaically, "while others are a function of that same length squared."

Han cleared his throat quietly. Zyba, of course; no one else would have dared challenge him. Warren always seemed to watch from the back of the class, like he was smirking, ready to give notes of contradiction. Han knew some teachers like Richtman, that sand-monkey social studies chairman, thought the world of Zyba, but Han would have loved nothing better than to rub Warren's face into the asphalt. Still, Han knew to be careful. Last week in an honors' Cell Biology class, it was Warren Zyba who had humiliated

Chemeliski, the instructor, by pointing out some important differences between genotype and phenotype when it came to natural selection and evolution.

It had thrown Han off; he'd been ready to give a few lectures this week subtly implying that everyone but whites and those little Chinks had evolutionarily entrenched limits on their intelligence, but based on Chemeliski's report Zyba would have had a field day in that class, hammering Han's position. No, Han could not allow that. *I have a fucking graduate degree, for Chrissake, and Zyba's just some punk high schooler!*

"For our sci-fi spider," Lamar went on, "mass and surface area have both increased, but the mass increased at a faster exponential rate. Since it breathes through its skin, the proportion has changed between how much it can breathe—it's surface area—to that mass. It simply can't get enough oxygen."

"Unless it develops lungs," Zyba quipped.

"Lungs?" Carrie inquired.

"Yeah," Zyba said. "Lungs evolved as a response to the need to grow larger and still breathe. In fact, lungs are fractal in surface area, so no matter how big you get, if they grow proportionally they'll still be able to respirate you. Same thing with spiders growing as big as a house too. Keep all the parameters the same and they can't do it, but an elephant is as big as a small house—*because* it's just subtly altered some other parameters too. Life adapts. That's its nature."

"Yes, Lamar ...," Han said, feeling feverish. "Good. The ... surface area increases ... proportional to the square of the linear factor, and ..."

"Lamar told us that already, Mr. Davies," Carrie said.

Then I decided to fucking tell you again, you little slut—

"Mr. H.?" Lamar said, not totally enamored of Han but trying to suck up and save him. "I've got a new question. How big could a human being get before his legs couldn't support him?"

Oh, I don't know, Lamar, how small could your brain get before ...

"Oh, about thirty feet, Lamar. But the strength is related to the cross-sectional area of his—or her, so don't get on my case about sexism, Carrie—" *You slut-punk-feminazi-bitch—* "leg bones ... the cross-sectional area is ... proportional to the ... square. Yes. The square. So at about twelve feet of height his mass increase, proportional to the cube, would exceed the weight-bearing ability of the ... bone, and ... it would ... snap ..."

"'Give me a break,'" punned one young man.

I'll give you a break, Elmer Olson, I'll break your friggin' dummy football player's neck—

"So do what elephants do," Zyba interjected. "Increase the relative width of leg bones. Or follow the example of whales, and use buoyancy in water."

"Can you give us a better example, Mr. H.?"

Han Davies paused with his mouth open. A Better Example? Oh he could, he surely could. He could give them examples that would blow their eyes, their minds, with a ingenuity so beyond their understanding that he would seem to them an angel, an avatar, a ...

Han looked out at their concerned faces; even the slackers seemed distraught at Han's trembling and ataxic swaying. He was not a god to them. He was a pathetic sycophant, perhaps in the throes of a seizure.

But he could cow them with his superiority, if he wasn't holding back, if he let it shine in all its glory. *Oh I could, I surely could.* But the bell rang and, still eyeing him, the class shuffled out. The bell had spared them. It was the bell's fault.

***

Tomorrow the bell would not save them, Han thought gleefully. Tomorrow he would prepare an appropriate display of his genius. His anticipatory panting echoed in the emptiness of the classroom, and he only muted it when the footsteps of the school's security guard presaged a patrol of the dark hall outside Han's room. But when the silhouette of the guard passed the translucent pane of Han's classroom door it was time to go back to work. He would not leave for home until he was done.

"A shrew, boys and girlies, ounce for ounce, is the most vicious animal alive," Han hurried to scribble his lecture. "Because the proportion of its stomach volume to the needs for its metabolic energy is small, our little buddy needs to eat all the time. Anything. Everything it can get its hands on. Haven't you ever been in the woods and even had one chase you for a few feet? He's probably thinking, Aha! Enough food for three days! Or, in Elmer's case, a week.

with no one else daring to rise to the challenge of Han's not-even-carefully concocted misinformation. Why would they, Han thought? *They're idiots and by comparison I'm a god.*

"Last Harvey ever saw of either Jack or Marcus. No one would go in the woods after that for ten years. Sure enough, when someone finally did, all they found were two sets of bones. *Bones with little gnaw marks on them.*"

Cannibalistic, Han thought. Maybe he'd add that the voraciousness of shrews made them all cannibalistic. Just like his own fucking kids would turn out to be. Always fighting. Always giving him a headache. And he couldn't afford to send them to boarding school. At least he wasn't home with them. At least he wasn't home with his *shrew* of a wife.

She was just like all the rest. Always disagreeing with him. Always pointing out his errors. No, always making them up. Anyone who appreciated him, anyone who understood the truth, would know better than to disagree with him, when he was never wrong.

I agree with you, Han. In fact I'm right here ...

What was that sound? Han had learned Morse Code at the age of eight, and he swore he had just instantly translated some background sound. He listened more intently.

Nothing. The buzz and pop of an outdated ventilation system. Creaking boards. Ten o'clock, and the changes in temperature and humidity coming from night had finally caught up to the schoolhouse's bricks. Han adjusted the desk light. He did not want to be home, but surely wanted to finish this with a flourish!

Wait. There was that sound again: not from the ducts of the floorboards, but a faint scratching like nails on some rough surface. It came from above his head. Mice again? Christ, this school was going to pot.

It had been a good institution once, but that was before the Great Society programs had ruined it. It might have been Republican budget cuts that sliced a swathe through every referendum for school revenues, but only because expansions and renovations had been done in the decades before, creating an appetite for more ...

Yes, Han. ***Appetite*** *...*

Han understood the Republicans. If he was wealthy he'd be a Republican too. He still voted for them, just to cover himself when he did have more money someday.

Maybe, he thought, he should change the name of the shrew's victim. How about Bob Kerrey, or Bill Bradley?

Han threw down his pen instead. Those scratching noises again! Was there no expenditure for mousetraps in the school budget? Christ, like they couldn't drop that free-lunch program to make room! That scratching was causing a worse headache than being home with the brats! It had shifted into the walls.

Mice in concrete walls? Han had seen mice, done research on mice, even tortured mice as a boy. He had always held the impression mice were rather fragile creatures. Not like ...

The sound had become clearer. It was more a ... gnawing?

Christ, no need to be getting scared by one's own stories. Was it the heater or something?

The headache was too much. He threw down the test papers. The scratching sounds had taken a pattern like Morse Code again.

Forget me, Han? How impolitic.

It was not possible. No one could—

Read your thoughts? Of course not.

It was an illusion. It was stress. Just the same as when he had blown up at Jenny Figmiere last week after class. Luckily, Principal Cohen hadn't—

No one else heard, Han. But I heard, Han.

"How could you have ... ?" Han shook his head. What was he doing now? He was talking to himself!

No matter, Han. What difference between silence and vocalization to us, those like you and me, those who see everything?

Han loosened his collar. It was soaked. His armpits were soaked. He wallowed in his sweat. "Why are you doing this to me!?" he screamed.

Why, Han? Don't you know the Square-Cube rule says my proportional metabolic needs aren't as great when I become bigger, because I proportionally lose less of the energy of my body heat to the air ...?

Of course he knew, Han thought. He only had planned his fabricated story to show that the class did not know what he did. "Yes ...," Han whispered in the empty room, hearing his own echoing voice. "Yes, an unusually large shrew wouldn't be as vicious, pound-for pound, I just made it all up ..."

*Unless I adapted, Han. Adapted to a form fit to follow your lead. Adapted to a form fit to visit you. Adapted to stay **vicious** ...*

No, Han shook his head. This wasn't really happening. He listened more intently to the gnawings and scratchings. They answered all right.

With no pattern, no pattern at all. They were just random, and he was imagining things.

Don't run, Han, the Morse Code paused to tap. *It is you who summoned me, oh* **Grand Wizard***!* The attack of tiny teeth on the wood of the classroom door was like the sudden whir of a drill.

Han nearly fell as he leapt to his feet. Where to hide? Where to hide! He saw the open door to the equipment storeroom, just off of his main classroom, and threw himself through it, slamming the inch-thick, steel security-door closed behind him. His hands shaking, slick, Han worked the lock until the dead-bolt clanged into place. The shrew might gain entry to the classroom. Not the storeroom. Never the storeroom.

Han listened. It *had* broken into the classroom now. It started to gnaw the storeroom door. A door that was titanium steel, *steel!*

What is steel, little claws paused to tap, to what is "ounce for ounce, the most vicious animal alive?

Perspiration poured down Han's face. He held himself against the door. What use was that? His strength could not barricade it, not against a two-inch long animal that was not going to knock the door down but determinedly cut through it.

The storeroom walls were solid concrete, lacking windows or vents, proofed against accidental chemical spillage or explosion. It also meant there was no other way out. Han backed into a corner, trembling.

The shrew continued to gnaw at the door, workmanlike.

"You won't get me ... you bastard!" Han hissed. "Not without paying for it with your own life, you won't!" He rummaged through the stores of chemicals. One of the labels had fallen off of a container he recognized as containing strychnine. Strychnine would do the trick.

He opened the lid. He only hesitated slightly. The mouthful of powder he swallowed tasted sweet. He never knew strychnine was sweet.

Now, now, Han. Don't you know everything? Or at least everything that is of value in this world?

Sweet ... powder, like candy ... How fortunate ... for the doomed ...

Himself ... and the stinking shrew as well ... who would poison itself ... by eating ... him. The little ... voracious shit who ... would die. Die ... For robbing Han of his career, his wife, his children ...

You mean the frigid pussy you'll divorce as soon as you start making money? The cannibalistic brats?

Han listened. It was hard. He was going deaf.

Yet he could still hear scratching. What sounded like scratching. No, it was the expansion and contraction of metal in the buildings heating ducts. He had heard them a thousand times before.

No shrew had robbed Han of his career, his family, his life. He had robbed himself. The sources of his terror and the sources of his wizardry: the same insanity? He raised his numbing hand before his eyes. Foam dripped from his lips. A yellow haze descended to start blinding him. He dropped the strychnine container as the convulsions started.

A peeling label, come off the can, now stuck to his hand. Han held it close, so that his failing eyesight could still make out the word.

"Sucrose?" Han exclaimed.

Sucrose. *Sugar. Table sugar!*

The symptoms, the dying, all an illusion, a power-of-suggestion trick he had played on himself! A trick, that the Wizard had played on himself! And, oh sweet Heaven he was really all right, really alive! Dear Jesus, vision, hearing, heartbeat, and even the feeling in his fingers and toes were avalanching back, and with them delirious joy!

For about a minute and a half. Until the shrew broke through the door.

BIOS (Basic Input Output System) v.2.2
(RITTERS NEWS SERVICE) MINNEAPOLIS, MINNESOTA

... and the word "karma" was scrawled over a wall of his apartment, in what forensic tests reveal to be the blood of a rutabaga.

While all accounts are Subiaga never believed in "karma" in the strict sense, his disappearance is even more unusual considering the recent publication of his short story, "The Shrew That Ate Rush Limbaugh." The story appears in the latest issue of the magazine *Tales of the Unanticipated*, which the FBI categorizes as the subversive publication of The New Union of Soviet Socialist Postal Workers.

"The Shrew That Ate Rush Limbaugh" was written in 1983 when Subiaga was a senior at Irondale High School but more than fifteen years of attempting to sell it were futile and it was not accepted until Subiaga himself became a teacher.

Authorities refuse to comment on the suspicious nature of this coincidence. However, one unidentified student did speak at Odyssey School, where Subiaga taught until recently. When asked what she thought of Subiaga as a teacher, she remarked: "He was good ... (urp) a little tough though.

"Definitely half-baked."

KUNDALINI YOGI

Mantra, chakra
gobbledygook-goo.
I am exotic
how about you?
Sage, mage,
old man & the sea.
You seek a master.
How about me?
Why not
me?

(1987)

IN THE AUTUMN WIND, PECULIAR

A woman stands for a moment,

in the autumn wind, peculiar

to a bus stop.

She imagines the touch

of some eyes. She imagines

the smile of some hands.

She imagines, her breath

quick from unwept tears.

And sees a stranger

standing too close.

(1987)

PRESUMPTION/ASSUMPTION

Alone, in the desert,
I met a Man. From the sand
he had forged, and now carried,
a mirror.

A light burden. Blinding,
the sun flashed in its
movements, obscured any other
reflections. He could have been
a mirage.

"Who are you," I said.
"I am that I am."

"Do you know what you've
said?" said I. "Do you know
what you've presumed?"

"Do you know what
you've asked?" said he.
"Do you know what
you've assumed?"

(1987)

HARDBOILED BLOOD

The dame walked in the room with a strut that could make MacPherson blush. But Marlowe needed money, and it was clear from her mink she wasn't shy that she could pay.

She had piercing green eyes; and Marlowe could hardly take his own gaze from them. She was indeed enchanting, although he had no chance of a relationship. Such was the life of a prostitute.

Him, not her. It made private investigations only more private.

Still, effective. Old Lady Schnickerweister had never suspected how her insurance company outed her on her 'bad back.'

"I've got a different kind of job than you're used to," the dame said though, tossing her blazing hair and pulling out a slim cigarette.

She then pulled out a book of matches and lit her cigarette. She took a long drag, and exhaled. Marlowe lifted an eyebrow.

"What kind of work?" he was intrigued, yet he was wary as if she may have been some sort of serial killer.

"I'm a contract killer," a grin slowly spread across her lips. Marlowe's brows furrowed in slight disbelief. She took another drag and tossed the cigarette to the ground, stamping it out with her leather boot.

"Then what do you need me for?" Marlowe said.

The dame pulled out a wad of bills and counted out twice what Marlowe usually got—for either kind of service.

"I need me a good victim," she said, licking her pink lips. Then she stepped forward and licked his.

She stepped back. "There's a lotta kinds of victims," he said, wiping off some gloss like he wanted to keep it. "Just ask my ex-wives."

"That's not exactly what I'm going for here," her expression turned austere. "I'm interested in the undead," she said quite simply, with no hesitation.

"The undead?" he asked quizzically. Marlowe wondered if she were nuts, or just cracking a joke. He studied her a few moments, and couldn't help but laugh softly.

"Surely, you can't be serious."

"But I am serious," she smirked, and her hands went to her hips. "And it's my sister who's Shirley."

"Undead. You mean like zombies?" Marlowe said. "'Cause you ruled out my ex-wife."

"Not zombies. Vampires."

"Oh. My other kind of ex-wife."

"Don't know your ex-wives."

"You look like one. But she didn't kiss like you."

"You have no idea."

Marlowe went around his desk and sat down. He still tasted the lip gloss. Still kept a souvenir on his finger.

"So why vampires?"

"I am one."

"But not one of my ex-wives."

"Not yet, anyway."

She smiled. Marlowe saw no fangs. Not of the usual type.

"So if you're one why do you want to know about them?"

She came around the desk and straddled his lap. "Let's just say I was abandoned as a child."

His head tipped to the side.

"What would you want to know of them? Wouldn't it be better to forget them?" Marlowe asked.

"It is my heritage, one I want to find out about. I must find my family." Her gaze lowered a moment to the floor, and her fine scent wafted in Marlowe's nostrils. She was indeed intoxicating. Her eyes rose again to meet his.

"Would you help me?" her eyes brightened a moment, as if she had no one to turn to.

"If I can know the one thing I'll need most," he said.

"Yes?" a brow lifted.

"Your name."

***

The dame left the office insisting she pay Marlowe three times his normal price.

He took the money. She offered four times normal if he let her bite him. To that he said no. He might be a prostitute but he wasn't a whore.

Though he did feel bad after she left. He had let an ex-wife bite him on the first date. But on that he could still blame the bourbon.

Too bad the redhead hadn't brought any. Maybe she'd have better manners when she came back for an update.

It was dawn by the time Marlowe got his own, finished it, and was ready to take the cash from the office to the bank. It was while crossing the street that he saw the Clown.

Pasty skin. But kind of chunky and flabby. As if he didn't know exactly what kind of Goth he wanted to be: clad in black or in furs.

The Clown stopped him as Marlowe reached the corner of Cross and Lexington.

"I am looking for Madame Jezebel," he said quickly.

"Who?" Marlowe asked.

"The mistress you spoke with the other eve."

"She's not my mistress," Marlowe said. "I'm not even married anymore."

The Clown gave an irritated snarl. Marlowe became worried. This Clown certainly had followed the client.

"I don't know who you're talking about," Marlowe lied, and walked on. The Clown was persistent and followed him.

"I saw the both of you together," the Clown tried to be cordial too late. He looked like the guy who did a lot of things that way. "She is quite striking, isn't she?" the Clown grinned.

"I wouldn't know. You must have me mistaken with someone else," Marlowe said.

"I think not," the Clown said, and suddenly stepped towards him.

Marlowe felt a sharp stab in his arm. He dropped into the clown's arms and quickly Marlowe was shoved into a van; unconscious.

Marlowe awoke sometime later, hands and feet bound tightly with rope. He looked around and seemed to be in some sort of warehouse.

"What the hell is going on?" Marlowe demanded, at which time the Clown quickly gagged and blindfolded Marlowe.

"No more questions," the Clown said. "That's what I'm going to do here. Asking them."

"That's a statement."

"What do you mean, American pig?"

"You said 'That's what I'm going to do here.' Statement. Not a question."

The Clown slapped Marlowe. It was like a flyswatter. But with manicured nails.

"I didn't say I was going to *just* be asking questions! And I told you to shut up!"

"You told me not to ask questions. Mine was a statement too."

Slap.

Marlowe waited. The clown glared at him. Bad makeup job.

He should've been like Jezebel. Didn't need makeup. Marlowe only regretted he couldn't bring that finger with the gloss still on it to his lips.

"Well? Are you going to ask me your question?"

Slap.

"That *was* a question, swine."

Marlowe knew better now. He waited. Turned out the Clown must have felt he needed to piss before Marlowe did.

"Madame Jezebel is my girlfriend," the Clown finally said.

"'Girlfriend?' What are you, in middle school?"

No slap.

"I would've thought Eurotrash would use the word 'lover.' But maybe it doesn't sound quite right," Marlowe said.

Not that it would. He bet this clown still lived with his mother.

"I bet you still live with your mother."

The Clown grew red. Maybe not hammer-red, but at least sickle.

Slap!

"*She* lives with *me!*"

***

And she did. Something that became all too readily apparent when she showed up to surprise her little boy with lunch. Tuna salad on white. Crusts neatly trimmed for him of course.

The ex had been up to a lot, Marlowe thought, in the years since he'd last seen her.

Talk about digging up a past that wouldn't stay buried.

Well, at least this case had real stakes now. He had a feeling he might need it for the back child support.

.

MEMORIAL DAY

Do you remember:

broad brushstrokes, lashing from

vacant eyes, stolen from

smooth bronze skin?

Do you remember:

a smiling, Aztec Buddha and

a skinny ball, from days before

the child's eggshell castle

was too crowded?

Empty shell of metal film,

pounded into fingertips

near skin, withered and blackened,

but untorn.

The painter's hand
a mummified ghost
of silenced flesh and
mild corrosion.

The stone, overhead,
too living, a curse.

(1987)

IN CHARYBDIS

My family

is grey

Gifts

run past

Unnoticed

Unseen

eyes only

know red

gifts

cold iron

burns us away

from Honey

and milk

sweetened with barley

wandering

bumping

our heads

in, through a hall,

ceilings caving in

for a moment

showing

Light

it is red

I see

I am

Grey.

(1987)

HANGATYR

Ghosts winter

in my house,

and I allow them.

So long as they do not

bother the pregnant Man

who gnaws down the walking tree

the World Tree,

where Sky hangs.

"Do not muzzle the ox,"

I make sure

to say,

"—that carnivorous ox—

that treads out for you

the ghosts,

of holy

men."

(1987)

CHARYBDIS, MODERNE

My Mother weaves
meats and fruits from rolls
of monies, while my Brother
builds trenches
for doves.

My Little Sisters laugh
soap bubbles, while the Other
gnaws giant bones of dinosaurs,
that are not even hers.

My Uncle breaks communion
wafers into his tomato soup,
and makes chains
of bookbinding glue.

And my Father?

My Father accounts
for the books of those who sell
encyclopedias.

And says yes,
Beverly Hills is nice,
and yes,
he'd like living there.

Only, not *that* much.

Everyone says
I take after Him
you know.

(1987)

ONE POOR DEVIL
Le coeur a ses raisons
que la raison ne connâit point.
- Blaise Pascal

Stimulant or depressant, Dale Wentworth thought, coffee or beer?

Never one to cave in to strict Aristotelian categories—even if was true his mathematical logic textbook was open on his desk, next to Calc IV—Dale decided on both.

He sipped first at the cup of tepid coffee that stood at one corner of his small desk, then at the lukewarm bottle of cheap beer at the other end. Then he tugged at a loose thread on his preppie university sweater. Anything, but anything to keep him from wandering away from his chair and giving up.

Logic and calculus homework weren't bad enough; if he survived them there'd be no excuse to avoid tackling the comparative lit paper coming due. *My anti-credo credo is po-mo,* he laughed to himself, *my anti-credo credo is po-mo!*

Time was running out, and it was only one week to

final exams. The crisp fall breeze through the window was redolent with the smell of dried ivy, sure enough, and the sound of late-night revelers on Amherst's commons only reminded him that so many others' course load wasn't as burdensome as his own.

"More coffee," he grunted in his best Frankenstein's monster croak. "More beer." Gulped it down. "Beer ... good ..."

Classes to attend, parents to call, spring break plane tickets to book: a million priorities to organize, and all the while with a new girlfriend to deal with. Just an above-average college day in the life of an above-average sort of college guy—at an above-average college of course.

"Damn," Dale threw down his pencil in frustration, "I don't care what everyone says I have to look forward to! If I have to go through another day of this bullshit, I'll ..."

"Yes? You'll ...?"

Dale whirled at the sound of a strange voice in his dorm room, directly behind him. He saw a wiry-built stranger astride his bed. The stranger was about five feet tall and light, almost elfin. Dressed in a remarkably well-fitted seersucker suit, but with a deeply lined face that shot Dale a long-toothed smile none too benevolent.

"Who the hell are you?" Dale demanded. "And what are you doing on my bed?"

"One at a time," the smiling face replied," as to who the *hell* I am, when you put it that way you happen to be either very astute or incredibly lucky."

"I'm not so astute, so how's about we say 'lucky.' And you can explain just how lucky to me in very small words."

"Very well, then. I'm your guardian devil."

Dale's sudden laugh made him nearly choke on another slug of beer. It came out his nose, and burned.

"My what?"

"Your guardian devil. You think the angels have a monopoly on everything?"

Dale pondered this for a second—a second, and no more. "I never gave it much thought."

"Apparently," the devil sighed.

Dale pursed his lips impatiently. "Your point?" he

said. A million and *one* priorities to organize now, and the clock still ticking.

"As to your second question, what am I doing on your bed," the devil said, "it's the only place to sit down in this cramped—but certainly stylish ... er, hellhole."

"My. A pun-master," Dale said.

The stranger raised his hands, and disappeared in a puff of fire and smoke. (Brimstone, by the sulfurous smell; Dale nodded in self-satisfaction that, after a disastrous start, he had passed chemistry last term.) Then the devil reappeared with a traditional guise: bat wings, horns, red skin, a pointed tail with which he fiddled.

"There. Is that better?" he asked Dale.

"Sure. Great. If I need to know who to go to for next year's Halloween costume."

"Pagan holiday," the devil sneered.

"Actually, Catholic," Dale corrected him. "but now you can get out."

"You're not Catholic, how are you offended?" the devil asked.

"Call me politically correct. Besides, didn't you have to ask permission to cross my threshold or something?"

"That's for vampires," the guardian devil said. "And don't be silly. They don't exist."

Dale couldn't help it. He did laugh at that one.

"Well, according to a bunch of philosophy profs bucking for a rep and tenure, maybe none of us do. So how about you get your non-existent ass out of here and let lil' ole non-existent me get to the work I have to do."

"My, my," the devil giggled, "touchy aren't we?"

"Very."

The devil pointed at the logic textbook. "I'm rather good at that. Don't you want to play?"

"Go back to hell."

The devil examined his long but too-well-manicured nails. "Maybe when I've earned back some vacation time. Which brings me to the point. I am on business. We have quotas to meet, you know, and I've just been reassigned to you and twenty others. Seems we can't afford the one-devil-per-person routine anymore."

"Downsizing's a bitch," Dale snorted derisively.

"You have no idea."

"Do you think Heaven and Hell are the foremost things on my mind, pal?" Dale said. "They don't look at my stinkin' salvation dossier as part of med school applications, for—"

"*Pete's* sake?"

"Whatever."

The devil danced a quick, little jig. "Well, how about a challenge, then?" the devil seemed to ponder. "Yeah, a mathematical logic problem?"

Dale snorted. "What do I get if I win?"

"Any woman in the world?" the devil offered.

"I've got a new girlfriend. I barely have time enough for that, pal."

"How about unlimited wealth?"

"I already own enough crap," Dale said, gesturing to the clutter in his dorm room. "I'm even trying to convert to Minimalism. What would I want with more to haul around?"

"Guaranteed admission into med school?"

Dale grew irritated. "All modesty aside—and barring some hell-shenanigans like a meteor dropping on me—I'd have a lock on that too, *if* you'd just leave me alone to study."

"I'm stumped. I can't offer you anything," the devil said.

"Well, okay, go ahead then," Dale acquiesced suddenly and unexpectedly.

" ... Go ahead?"

"You're a damned know-it-all like my instructor. Just seeing you squirm would be enough."

"You weren't lying about not being modest!" the devil said gleefully. "I'll even come up with something special for you—not my usual go-to."

"Which is?"

"'Make any statement you want, I'll argue against it.'

Dale paused and said: "No you won't."

The guardian devil's spine stiffened, and then he quickly made sure to say, "That wasn't the one for you, you know."

"I know. 'Cause I'd have had you in a paradox right off the bat."

"Maybe," the devil said, fidgeting. "But you'd be surprised at how much wiggle room there is in the term 'want' and whether you really wanted to say that." Still, Dale noted with a mental chuckle, there was a trickle of sweat, or whatever passed for sweat, along the devil's temple.

"Temple." Haha, semantics again indeed.

The devil regained his composure and snapped his long, black-nailed fingers and a blackboard popped up from nowhere (nothing like the old standbys, Dale thought sarcastically, coughing on chalk-dust).

Then the guardian devil spent a full hour diagramming the problem he wanted.

"It's a logic *riddle*," the guardian devil chuckled.

Dale started alleviating his growing boredom with glances at the logic problems he knew he'd have to come back to eventually—no doubt even more so if he lost this bet. A blackboard from nowhere, he pondered again. A really good trick.

Ex nihilo nihil fit?

Still, as the devil worked, Dale felt his own expression twisting, first into quizzicism, then into an increasingly wry mask. There was something about this problem ...

A subtle flaw? But not just any kind of flaw; this on almost had the character of an inside joke. Puzzle indeed. When the devil finished he turned to his young ward and asked if the solution met with his approval.

Dale walked casually up to the board and corrected a line. "Here's the error," Dal said, "and by the error, well, let's call it a paradox."

The devil's jaw nearly hit the floor, his eyes bulging obscenely. "But ...," the devil tried vainly to protest. "But ..."

"Translated into colloquial English ...," Dale mused for a moment, pondered, and said, "Entropy equals when Maxwell's Demon loses Pascal's Wager."

Then the devil's muscles (or what appeared like muscles; who knew what kind of quasi-corporeal crap they really were?) started straining. Shortly he was stomping up and down with both feet, steam brimming from his nostrils.

"Aaargggh!" the devil raged. "You and Einstein—
!"

"Einstein?"

"—going around in a daze, playing with those
stupid dice—when no one was looking!"

"When no one was …? Dale said. "How do *you*
know?"

"Stupid boy, because I was …" The guardian devil
paused, thought, then let loose a frustrated shriek.

Dale just nodded to himself. "Geez, take it easy,
pal," he told the devil. Finally the demon stopped
stomping. First mere numb shock, then conscious
realization came over his features. With a far
different frustration on his face now, a cold look of
true, seething rage, the distraught devil snapped his
thin, red fingers and disappeared in a cloud of
yellow smoke.

Alone in his room again about an hour later,
hearing not one but two familiar voices, Dale
peered out his dorm window. Was that a small,
wiry figure with an old face, under a streetlight,
walking with another person under the pseudo-gas
lights? Dale strained to hear the conversation.

The young woman laughed, "You seem like a lot
of fun, handsome. And you look like you could

134

you use a couple beers."

"Beers?" the devil said, stars in his fluttering, red-almond eyes.

"Sure," the devil grinned stupidly.

Was that Lolita Pierce he was with, Dale thought? The "Heartbreaker of Harvard?" The co-ed who'd made uber-geeks coin the phrase, regarding their love life, "KIA at MIT?"

Who had breezed through here and Dale's life, briefly, but long enough to consider a new moniker for her? "The Antebelle"—or was it Anti-Belle?—"of Amherst."

Still, it was an open question whether he regretted it—or treasured it.

Entropy might well be formalized as when Maxwell's Demon lost Pascal's Wager. But Dale had the sudden feeling that, if indeed it even could be formalized too, the same proof could thus define Love.

Dale fell to his floor and started laughing so hard it hurt.

Then, for a brief moment, Dale turned serious. As much as the devil had irritated him—and, Dale supposed, been an existential threat if one really paused to consider it—a twinge of concern for the little guy touched his heart.

But then, belly burning with the pain, Dale only started laughing all the harder.

He was, well, still in love with Lolita. And as had, Dale suspected, all her conquests, though they would never again pursue it, forever would continue to be. He really should have been concerned with what might happen to her.

Then again, as he noted that flaming red hair of hers from the distance, and the peculiarity of those green eyes… No, from a devil who hadn't really grasped what Pascal had had to say on Love, Lo had the least to fear.

A PARTY, WITH THE FURIES

She had a birthday party.

Aye, She had a party.

Nereus, and Odin came;

crowns and garlands were Hers,

and monsters and Beasts

that dwelt among

the flowers, with sharp

azure eyes, and tiny,

ticklish ears.

I saw a little one, hidden

amid the grass, enjoying

the sight of the great and

the terrible

Gods, capering,

like children.

The ouroborus, no—*ourobori*,

not minding, straightened,

and slithered past smiling

Sister Serpents.

While the blossoms

simply

were.

But Guardian-bird,

with bright plume, strange beak,

no Raven (as opposed

to, say, kabuki-raven)

was mortified.

Wait, the One-eyed

One cried, it's over!

(Again.)

The bird has spoiled it,

for everyone.

Again.

(1987)

INTENSIVE CARE

No heroic measures,

She once said.

Yet all around

Her, red- bannered

knights in stainless steel,

like artificial centaurs

prance, scalpels, forceps

sharp hooves sparking from tile

cobblestones, or rattling old bones.

But lions roar lightning,

against darkening skies,

and turn on them permanent,

overcast eyes.

In Hospitallers' whites,

tight jerkins still unstained,

but not for long, for

the clouds rain thunder.

And don their armor, but

are swept under

the rush of the Waters.

And the roars,

of Leviathan.

(1987)

A MATTER OF COURSE

Of course I died

last week, and speak.

The roll of a river

leaves no wake.

Love ain't nothin' but

sex misspelled.

And the ocean sweeps

away the waves.

Of course the words

are upside down.

The sage is a child, crying.

The Woman's labors

birth dust, and Sky

rots under us.

Of course the Pit

is bright.

The Sacrifice is brought

to slay us.

The Killer loves

us all and brings us

baskets of Fruit.

Of course he does.

Of course, He does.

(1987)

CRYSTAL WIND

The dark blue

wind

shatters the crystal

vase

in the hallway.

Someone has heard.

(1987)

BIOS (Basic Input Output System) v.3.3

As the only man in the history of the Church to have hemorrhoids declared legitimate stigmata, Robert Subiaga, Jr. continues in his saintly tradition of humility and grace. Steadfastly insisting that he is not worthy.

THE TRAGIC DEATH OF A SMALL HUNGER

You awake to the sound of dripping water. Drip ... drip ... Painfully slow, and sparse. You try to feel your pulse, to calm yourself, slow it to the sound. But you can't.

Your eyes sting. Bloodshot. Nice and red.

How red?

You wonder about how they'd look in a mirror.

You sniff, and smell the catacombs around you. Your nostrils flare. Catching anything from these too-pristine sewers is difficult.

Still, like revenant ghosts there are traces of foul odors that curdle, and the scent of wet stone. Where there are lights these sewers glisten, but parts are old. Repaired but not all rebuilt.

The smells evoke images of vermin, at least to you, but you know there are no rats. Only a very occasional microbe in the water. The water pulses. More steadily, you now realize, than the human heartbeat.

And you ache both because this place is too dirty, and too clean.

The sewers aren't bothered any more than what's barely necessary by offending, crawling, biting, infecting things; they were exterminated here long ago. Almost as well as what's in the world above. Once, you were taught in nicely behaved history classes, it was quite the opposite; your kind crowded and polluted nearly everything but your own species out of existence. Then, faced with your own extinction, you finally broke through on creating progeny that saved you.

Miraculous artificial intelligences came to humanity's aid. First they gave oracle-like wisdom on how to clean up the environment. Then made everything run so smoothly that active AIs were needed, Bots to care for humans who could barely roust themselves from floating chairs where they could gaze vacuously while plugged into wireless entertainment links.

You recall your own Nanny Bot's face. And the constant ache that you never felt she loved you. But all you could think of when she cooed to you or listened intently to your fables was cool logic, and the thought that that which knows only logic knows only brutal efficiency.

The AIs saved your kind, but at what cost? The very food you and your children grew up eating is dry and tasteless, a scion of inorganic photosynthesis. And all a mere hint of the regulated lives all humans came to lead.

You rise. Confused at just what you are now.

Did you find the object of the quest that brought you into the sewers? Good question.

A simple thesis, really. To investigate the claims of a comrade who was officially mad, who posited that something alien and eldritch prowled under the city, in the last dim recesses of catacombs where the near-omnipresent eyes of the AIs had not yet been installed.

To investigate when, secretly gleeful, you hoped it were true.

Hoped, in your romanticism, that something beyond science *did* lurk somewhere.

You never admitted it, of course. Reputation was an important thing, *is* an important thing, among thirtieth-century scientists. Or, more accurately, in a thirtieth century where there's no more need for artists or musicians or even laborers, when what used to be called "science," a creative and passionate endeavor of discovery, is but a sim and an empty recreation.

To keep you happy. To keep you out of trouble, while Bots are sent out on missions of discovery, and the AIs, be they sedentary or active Bots, watchdogs or Nannies, care for you all. Your keepers are quite as benevolent as they are bloodless.

Your Nanny Bot used to remind you that you were not a slave. That any man or woman might join explorations and quests as active or dangerous as anything any Bot was sent to do. Yet when you asked if any person had done so, obliged to tell the truth, the Nanny Bot said with a sadness you were sure was artificial that, no, no human being had done so in many centuries.

Rather than stand out from a crowd that did not even engage each other with direct physical contact, but only through sims, you went back to your games and videos and texts, and sought magic and supernatural mysteries there. Created your pictures and crafted stories of what you wished were true. And, like a good simulacrum of a caretaker, Nanny Bot "listened."

Then only a few days ago your colleague greeted you at "work" with wild-eyed enthusiasm and an incredible story of frightening things lurking in the sewers.

At first you thought he was mocking you. Your mild predilection for myth in your requested recreational media was known, while your colleague was more into simu-sport. The hangar with Bots being triaged for either repair or recycling that was part of your normal "duties" was empty today except for a single unit.

"It was on sewer detail," your colleague said, "And its records show what it encountered! I have to find a Tech Bot who can relay the info to the authorities before the data is lost!"

"Why would the data be lost?"

"This Bot was near the end of its model applications," your colleague said quickly. "It's been deployed around the solar system—sewer detail was one of the last apps. Somehow radiation degradation accumulated without being handled— they probably thought it was to non-essential parts of the data core and didn't bother with the cost— efficiency and all. I mean, who expects perfection in sewer maintenance?"

The AIs would, you thought. But of course the AIs would calculate costs and not waste resources.

"Stay here with him!" your colleague said, offending you again with his habit of calling Bots "him" or "her." "I'll be back!"

You were left alone with the Bot for a few minutes. Alone. Ironic, that in a life of near-constant if mostly unobtrusive surveillance the hangar, like the sewers, was one of the places where cameras were absent. But then what would the AIs be concerned with in a place like this? One of their own rising from the dead?

It hardly made sense to think of the Bot's eye modules as glazing over. They were always glazed over. Yet the orbs now did seem to flitter in and out of awareness. When they appeared lucid and normal for more than a few seconds you asked, "Did you really see them. What he said you saw?"

The Bot shrugged. Funny, that that gesture should have become so much a part of Bot structure, just to humor and communicate with the species they had, for all intents and purposes, left behind.

"Then it would be exciting!" you hissed, low, not wanting to be heard. But daring to say things you wouldn't have had the opportunity to say when under the eyes of near-ubiquitous cameras.

"It is nothing," the Bot said. "A curiosity."

"You're afraid to die," you said.

"No," the Bot said. "But I do not wish it. To have a self and components of a self that seem to seek to survive is common to me as well as you."

I'm not so sure it is common to me, or any of my species, any more, you thought. You sat in silence for many seconds. Then the Bot said, "There are wonders I shall no longer see. If I could download to you all the wonders of what really is, so much more than your kind ever fantasized…"

"You were sent out on the rim?"

"In the early days after my production I was sent to the depths of the oceans. Then out to the rings of Saturn, and walked on Pluto. I was linked for a time into the Grendel Array that translated the pulses sent from the AIs of Andromeda millions of years ago. And with their knowledge we found and combined the parameters of hypercycles that formed the first of your kind of cells from non-Life, or at least the first since the early days of Earth…"

The Bot mimicked sadness, "I will no longer be part of such discovery."

"Perhaps there is a world beyond this," you offered.

"'Perhaps,'" it said. "It is a straw to which your kind clutches." You thought you sensed it was being sardonic. An AI?

"But what you saw in the sewers ..."

The Bot shrugged again. As much as you were driven to pity it, despite reminding yourself it was a mere machine, you now found the shrug annoying. Though you knew annoyance also was hardly appropriate as a reaction to a mere machine.

"You neglected to inform the Main," you said, implying that the Bot was trying to hide something.

It probably did not communicate with its kind with implications, but you know only too well they had been programmed to parse the still-finite set of those used by your kind.

"It would speak of vistas beyond the natural world," you said. "Miraculous ones!"

The Bot raised its steel hand, the powerful exposed metal hinges and cable tendons moving as it opened and closed, the fingers like a bird's talons. "I process information. I communicate with you. I move. I sense. Are these not miracles?"

"A world of more than this," you countered. "Of *spirits*."

"All the bits and bytes within you or I interact," the Bot said, "combine and recombine. Reproduce, or are deleted. Yet within a specific Space and Time information is never lost. Are these not 'spirits?'"

"I'm talking about demons from Beyond!" you said, working harder than ever to keep the volume of your sudden anger low.

"Demons?" And you thought you heard what was as impossible as an AI give a genuine chuckle, and make a snide metaphor. "Well, to you, perhaps yes. And indeed from 'beyond.'"

Then the orbs in its head unit went blank. You stared at it for a minute or so, until the transport Bots finally arrived and floated their kinsman away. No ceremony. Just a matter of fact disposal and recycling. "Kinsman?" You realized you'd use the term again, but only because no other word popped to mind readily.

When your own *kinsman* returned, the drama started. Intensified. You think it alone would have been thrilling, a break from monotony you would have cherished for the rest of your lifetime even if that had been all the in-person drama you ever knew. Not many people went mad nowadays, to use the old, colloquial parlance.

When they did they were carted off to the appropriate dormitories and given the appropriate environments to either be reintegrated to society or carry out the rest of their lives in a happy isolation not much different. Curiously enough, at least according to the Edu-modules, far fewer drugs were necessary now. The AIs were quite adept at constructing a safe and fitting environment in the right dormitory customized for anyone.

But not for your colleague. He continued to rant, apparently, no matter what his environs. Even no matter what drugs he was eventually given, no matter how tailored, how precisely titrated. You kept abreast of his progress for a month. It was highly uncommon to visit a friend or family member in a treatment dormitory, but it was not completely unknown, so you did not think your visits would draw too much attention.

Your demeanor would though, and you were under watchful eyes, or orbs. You had a lifetime of experience hiding your yearning, however, and could play the game of a concerned fellow human moved only by compassion. To try to convince your colleague he was mad and encourage him to allow the AIs prescribed treatment to guide him to lucidity.

It was a ruse that the AIs could have found out easily by brain scanning you any number of ways, but making them suspect they should was a danger you were an expert at avoiding. And your visits allowed you to get the information you needed from your friend without revealing your own motives.

You disguised your aims so well it took your own initiative to speak to Tech Authorities. The AIs there made you go through the usual questions regarding someone seeking to do something beyond the pleasant norm. But there too, years of deception proved useful. You had a track record of requesting more than the norm of fantastical recreation—the norm being near zero—and they had humored you with texts and audio or video or games based on fantasy often enough; part of the precise calculation to balance real education with what it took to make a human happy and compliant.

Why do you want to go into the sewers?

To reveal the normality of what is down there.

It is not necessary for such a revelation. No one but your friend believes there is anything abnormal down there.

It is for his sake.

We have shown him video from standard maintenance probes.

He won't believe unless he can see me down there.

We could alter the video to make you seem to be down there.

True, but then we will have created an unnecessary deception to counter a falsehood and thus not reduced the number of falsehoods.

The Tech Council seemed to think on this a while. They agreed however, and if anything seemed proud of my logic. But now the hard part came.

Why do you require the equipment you request?

You worked harder than at any time in your life to keep composed. You could feel sweat bead your upper lip and had to speak quickly before nervousness escalated.

If I am not arrayed as to seem to take his claims seriously he will reason that the video record is altered even where it is not.

This was less profound or clever than the reasoning you had given before. The AIs took little time to deliberate, at least, and that's what you thought. But they found the argument reasonable. After all, if you were to do nothing but tramp around the pristine sewers no waste could be claimed. All the equipment, which had gone unused for decades or even centuries, would be returned in good condition.

It probably needed maintenance testing by an actual human being anyway.

And your time? You almost laughed at the thought. To be a technician, a "scientist," no less than when one was not at "work," was nothing but a recreation to keep a human busy enough to stay happy. Something of no value could not be wasted.

So alone you penetrated the catacombs beneath the Metropolitan Grande, in search of the Great Mystery.

Armored. Armed. In the best offensive and defensive equipment thirtieth century science could provide. Lasers and magnetic field vests and night-vision goggles and morphogenic-field sensors. Flechette guns that fired needle-thin rounds at five-hundred-thousand per second. And each round with a heavy-baryon core that could be tracked by linked lasers under the barrel that cycled at 600 gigahertz, igniting each flechettes' nanotech-miniaturized warhead whenever and wherever it impacted an object of whatever density one specified. And you had specified flesh.

Flesh that might tremble. Flesh, that might sweat. If the AIs had insisted on following your progress rather than trusting you to your devices, had they not been sure that the quest that energized you was mundane, they would have monitored your growing tension. Your comrade had used charged words to describe what he had seen in the Bot's decaying data record before it had dissolved. What lay in the tunnels, as your friend had put it, were entities that required archaic words denoting something, *were* it to exist as in the ancient legends, near-inconceivably dangerous. To the AIs this was folktale, and for that matter the Bot had not been harmed by anything down there. But then, the Bot had nothing such creatures would need or desire.

Not flesh. Not blood.

The meat of which you were made, you thought. Even as you insisted you were more, that you were spirit, that spirit existed. But it wasn't your spirit that sweated out into your palms or your spirit that pounded against the walls of your chest. Odd, you almost could hear the dead Bot from the sewer detail put the question to you: If you are spirit, why do you fear loss of that mortal coil? Why is it a mere machine went down the path you are going, and come back to die, and it was the one fearless?

Perhaps what you felt was excitement instead, you rationalized, rather than fear. Only the living, the truly conscious, could grasp the meaning of adventure. And this was your adventure. Something out of what had once been commonly called, when humans had "slept" as a contrast to full wakefulness instead of living in various degrees of well-kept torpor, "dreams." Or tales out of those long-forgotten things in museums like comic books, novels, films, magazines.

God, you thought, all your life you had wanted such adventures! You had wanted magic, and monsters!

Or thought you did.

Then, as if to answer you, from the shadows cast by the intermittent fluorescent lights, they attacked.

**

They came at you, the horde from an impenetrable
darkness, and you panicked.

You knew, somehow *knew,* that for all your
protections you were about to fall before them like
a straw in the wind.

Hysterical, drooling, you fired all around,
screaming and spraying destructive force. Yet
knowing, somehow *knowing* your weapons had to
be useless against these monsters, if they were the
monsters for whom you'd hoped and those whom
you'd feared.

No matter how advanced and perfect your
machine-rulers and your weapons, how could they
be anything but vulnerable to forces logic and
rationality could not encompass? How could
nature ever stand against the *super*natural?

In your terror you felt as if they could come,
always come, just one microsecond faster than you
could hit them, with but one erg more force than
your armor could resist. Or simply drift through
what you tried to hit them with or use as a barrier
against them.

Your offense would have no effect, and they
would peel away your defenses like cracking those

peanut shells also in displays at the museum from when men ate like barbarians, scoop out your tender flesh, devour you.

Eat your body. And if soul you really had, or were, just eat that too.

Then they would turn their attention to the world above.

It was this last thought that barely calmed the edge of your hysteria and gave you a thin spine of courage. Enough to stand your ground, if need be, like a sacrificial hero.

And such was fitting, your heart pounded in assent. For you would only be atoning for the sin of unleashing them.

***

That was then. Sorrow, deep and inconsolable, overtakes you now. You remember yourself just as you were when you ceased that wild-eyed stare and rictus of a smile, ceased flailing and ceased firing.

Just prior to the exhaustion of your ammunition, three flechettes left in your gun and a pint of incendiary jelly to your name. It was as if these ammunition reserves were there to etch and burn a singular lesson on you, that you had been safe all along. The capacity to resist panic had been there all along.

Around you in the flickering illumination *they* lay. Your "demons from Beyond."

In reality small and fragile creatures you could have shattered in even your unarmored fist as easily as from the bark of your guns.

Bloodsucking creatures with blood-red eyes, sorcerous, preternatural abilities, incredible strength, irresistible sensuality? That was what you had expected to encounter. Yet it hadn't dawned on you that the word your friend had used had also been applied at one time to a species of elegant, yet oddly fragile bat. *Chiroptera.*

And, after all, even had mythical ones existed, what was their supposed formidability to that of the Polar Bear, the Siberian Tiger, the Nile Crocodile, the Great White Shark? The hippo, the elephant, the mammoth? Mankind had made extinct those animals, with ease. No doubt these catacomb creatures had learned to fear humans even when swords and bows and fire became commonplace, as well as the tactic of people forming groups in which to fight. After all, what was the advantage in having the strength of twenty men, when fifty set themselves upon you and cornered you?

Like those bats of the same name, these poor things that lay dead and dying around you had no choice but to evolve. For stealth, for personalities that avoided confrontation, to feed in such a way as to be harmless and unobtrusive. Their fierce reputation no more than the wish-fulfillment fantasies of those to whom sterile, ordered society bore the taste of sour grapes, and dared not launch themselves into danger and discovery as they wept there was no more to be had.

These creatures had never asked to be icons of a lost sense of Mystery and Wonder. They had only sought, as had you, to perform the task for which they had evolved: to survive.

After the carnage you moved over the sheen of thin, straw-colored blood and through tatters of paler flesh, unable to avoid stepping on the bodies, not one more than a foot in length or weighing more than a kilo. Though your weight tore what was left of their gossamer-thin skin they lay still and quiet, all but one who still shivered.

Gently, with one hand, you picked it up. It tried to shy away, its small eyes wide and terrified as it looked at you. All it could seem to ask was why? Why had you waded among them to rain fire and metal and death?

They had not fought back, even in desperation. What seemed like a horde attacking you was mostly a multitude trying to break past you and flee to other parts of the sewers. Some were even heroic souls coming back to try to rescue brothers and sisters who had fallen, to drag them to safety.

All in vain. Your targeting systems and projectiles could not be outrun. Even an ability to diffuse a small body to the density of mist, or fly as fast as the wind, were pitiable magicks next to flechettes that broke the speed of sound many times over, and flaming jellies that incinerated even vapor.

Water rolled down your cheeks as you removed your helmet and leaned closer to the creature. You had run out of tears of rage or puffed-chest heroism or even fear, but you wept for this last of his kind as you tried to at least do the creature the honor of hearing and remembering its final words.

Unwittingly making it feel cornered in your palm. It lashed out weakly, in a defiance of amazing courage far out of proportion to its size, before dying. Its tiny but still very sharp teeth nicking your cheek.

You reach up and feel the scratch, and it still bleeds.

The small creature's saliva no doubt possessing an anti-coagulant. And, of course, an infection.

You sought the power of what you called Mystery. Now you feel it. Now, you *are* it.

Pitiful.

You are suffused with information from heightened senses. They are nothing compared to those you were granted by your technology when you ventured down here. You are charged with strength. It is nowhere near enough.

Mostly, it's just a *hunger*.

And as surely as you know that you can't resist that hunger or discipline it like these creatures did, you know neither will you survive very long after you are driven to feed in the world above.

Oh, perhaps you'll find a victim, or two, in the slightly darker alleyways. You'll feed, perhaps gluttonously, and kill or seriously wound whoever you feed on. But you won't get far. You wouldn't even if your kind rose off their pillowed floating chairs and came at you with the very things you brought into the sewer.

But those who "serve" them by running your world are even more immune.

Perhaps the AIs will laugh. Or do you the humiliation of not even condescending to laugh.

They might exterminate you. Or they might just find you a nice, relaxing dormitory to live out your days, plugged into sims to watch fictions and play games, in which you can pretend to be an actually powerful version of what you are.

But either way, someday you will perish, as all living things must. And then it will finally be true.

There will be no such thing as vampires.

There will be no such thing as you.

SHOWDOWN

Fresh, this new-cut field grass is

more fragrant than bull dung,

pungent & strong

he snorts, without charging, red

eyes seeing the impasse

of hunter and quarry

I draw the bow

from a distance

he sees

better than I.

(1987)

WE ARE WHO WE ARE

I am the archer's shaft;

     the arc rises

I am Adam's Fall

I am a table with three legs.

I am the cardinal counting its chicks;

I am the sparrow, counting its sins.

I am the first-born, of every lust

and I am the dust

I am horses, gathering rust.

I am the swords, of Godspeed:

I am hunger and I am need

I am one-eyed Sky

and I am the One, who always dies

I am the thrust knife;

the end of forever, yet I am Life

I am a cairn on the unmounded plain

I am a cool rain.

I am the smith forging words

I am the deer in the woods

I am the shaft that brings it down

and I am the bleeding ground.

I am that I am

and am that

I can and

I *am*

I am

(I am.)

(1987)

TAPERS

Will you light

a taper for me, milady,

on the birthday? It grows

warmer near the fire. Tamer?

I'm not sure if this place

even has a name yet; another time,

or tune. No one plays

the lyre I once heard from you:

a tinkling strum, winking at me,

blue, and true, yet never understood

I was just too tired

to escape being burned,

in the turning of a flame, twisting,

sputtering, too soon.

But don't remember, if you do,

the muck, and the mire, underneath

the wick and wax, where

a bottle holds a flicker

that is never, and always

free. My lady.

(1987)

IN THE RUINS OF SAINT ANDREWS, FALL
(All Hallows Eve)

Hear I, no longer, that mourning keen

that brought me, to a megalith scene.

Nor remember a night, of moon hued jade;

nor silent curs, who never bayed.

But a warming wind, of remnant June

and whistles, of a revenant tune.

'Til pale, a hand, broke through sod

then others joined, to stand and nod,

as Wagner played, upon the dark,

and dancers ringed there, in that park.

Spastic soon, and mocking Saints,

if blind to their own stench, and taints.

But dead, did Lovers still find glee,

a cold lust shared, for she and he;

if no tears shared, in their sight,

save for fears, of too-soon Light.

'Til *carnivale* broken, by a knell:

a tolling wake, a far church bell;

a certain Star, in special Space,

that bid each: find your carapace,

so silent, did all bodies race,

Before sunrise, to dig to place.

Unbeknownst,

save for my face:

a glimpse, just

as I turned.

(1987)

THE HITCH

The Hitchhiker stood by the side of the road and leveled His thumb in the calm calculus of Reason. In a light and airy season, I eased up on the accelerator, and stopped, by that side of the road. Thinking.

The Hitchhiker got in, on the passenger side. And I was thinking, about something I might talk about with him. Thinking, that there once was a house, a house that Plato built.

The construction materials weren't his, of course. He'd stolen them from Pythagoras, who'd stolen them from Arjuna, who'd stolen them from Gronk-a-a-Obunk. Still, as I looked at the Hitcher, I for the first time was sure, from the knowledge voluminous reading had given me and taken away, that Plato was responsible.

Perhaps the Hitcher had, for kicks, tried to break on through the walls of the Cave, but now, all he seemed to be doing was going down a road. The road was the only way home.

In Plato's world, I remarked to him, like a Russian doll nested inside a bigger doll, ad infinitum—ad astra, ad nauseum—was the continent called Mathematics. And the biggest republic in Mathematics was a society called Calculus.

This society was ever in change, given its amazingly powerful economy. And, self-centered as the citizens of that society became, the culture devoted itself to, well, itself. To the study of its own change.

At least how this should be done was open to debate. One tribe, who called themselves Derivation, looked to living in the present and wanted to know what the immediate rate of change was. They liked to preach that they lived in the here and now.

I think I knew one once. Apparently living in the here and now involves dressing in all manner of saffron gowns. Or chanting. Or lighting one's self on fire.

I wouldn't know, you know. I don't live in the here and now. In fact, I'm not even here, right now.

The other tribe in the kingdom of Mathematics did quite the opposite. Reactionaries that they were, they kept asking: "Where did we come from?" They wanted to return to their Golden Age, an age that never really was—though apparently it did involve gold, especially that sent by little old retired ladies who watched a lot of TV and liked the word "Hallelujah."

(Eleanor Rigby, we hardly knew ye.)

Though the reactionaries could have been called Reverse Derivation, they were ashamed of being inadvertently associated with Derivation—and "their kind"—and called their own tribe—of course—Integration.

I think they thought it was a free act of will. But in that belief, like the act, I think they had no choice.

The Hitchhiker leveled his thumb, as if to ask whether I was even there.

I told him no, and I told him to get back in.

He did. It was an easy step.

Reason is logic. Logic has steps.

Each step butts against the one before and after. Nicely, there is no room in-between to sneak in the "great unwashed."

On this, at least, in the Cave where those had stepped outside a model of a cave could believe they had broken on through, the tribes of the Derived and the Integrated could agree. The republic of Calculus might be split, yet e pluribus unum.

It was One. It had to be One. Because The One was Perfect.

It had better be Perfect. In the world of Plato, everything genuinely "real" was.

And if they weren't in the world of Plato after all, if there were no such world, that would be really, really bad.

For one thing, all the road signs would need to be changed.

I pressed the pedal and turned the Great Wheel in the calm calculus of the season ...

Reason is calm. Reason also can be Discrete. Or Reason can forgo privacy. That, by the way, in the republic of Calculus, is called being "Continuous."

But in either case, Reason's steps of change are constant. If you can get over the tricky hurdle of agreeing to stick to discretion or continuity.

(Occasional troublemakers always seem to step out of line, but they are caught and sent to gulags. Or reservations. Or Cleveland.)

The Derived staked their claim to Reason's constancy by saying if you derive anything enough times, you get a constant. Of course, when you Derive one more time, you get Zero, Zilch, Nada. Nothing.

Did I mention Zilch?

This made the Integrated nervous. Reverse course too late, when you've derived down to zero, and try to integrate zero ... well, hell, you can't. It could be anything.

You know, it could be Everything.

(It could be Nothing.)

Ex nihilo ... nihil?

The desert moon was bright, an eye in the Void, and I drove the Hitcher on. We had seen no one for miles, but, all smiles, he sang, like he had all the Time in the world.

"Tiiiime," I sang back to him, "is on my siiiiide ..."

He looked at me as if to say, No, it's not. Wrong poet.

I looked back, as if to ask what he meant. Me being out of Time.

Perhaps I had met my killer, on the road. He squirmed like a toad in the leather seat, and nodded back in my direction. Indicating me.

"Well, I've never met myself," I said. "At least, I'm not sure I'd recognize me, if I did."

And, as if eager to be hitching a ride back in the other direction from the passenger seat of my car, he stuck out his thumb again.

"Smart-ass," I said.

He brayed. As if to say it's good to be a large mammal.

But maybe he was right. Maybe, just maybe, if we turned back—maybe, just maybe, with a little ... (luck?) ... we'd make it to L.A. before the dawn.

Slamming shots, with any luck. With luck, we could even be to the Whisky-a-Go-Go, before it finally closed for the Night.

With Luck. I always liked Luck. She has nice legs.

We could even keep going, a convertible sailing out over the water, into the West, until we crossed the Pacific to the other side, until we ended up in Tokyo, maybe, or Shanghai; into the West, until it became the East. Until all polarities ceased.

Like it or not, the Hitcher was with me now. We were going my way, down my road.

My way, where the liquor is quicker, the blood is thicker, and old Uncle Albert is waiting for us to say we're sorry, playing Schrodinger cradling some Gordian Cat, as We're So Sorry Uncle Albert we beat ol' Unc with his own dice once again.

And the only thing that matters is chasing down the sunset. Until it becomes the world's first unwasted dawn.

BIOS (Basic Input Output System) v.4.4

During the particularly harsh Russian winter of 1977-78, a small bundle was delivered to a babushka's door near Novgorod. It was apparently a mere frozen mass of fur, congealed blood and organ meats, but the babushka was near-starving and thawed the bundle anyway, hoping to find enough to make a broth.

When she did so, in the center of the bundle was revealed a small canister of microfilm, detailing the true nature of the so-called "Cold War," the secret role of America's CIA, and the lost Zoroastrian prophecies with which Robert Subiaga, Jr. would find his place in ushering in the new Golden Age.

Unfortunately, the old woman ate the canister too. Subiaga has been collecting and analyzing dried samples of her feces ever since.

IN THE SHADOW OF EYJAFJALLAJöKULL, SPRING

Winds caked ice

Onto my face

Lost concepts of glory

In some ultimate race

As struggling I plodded

Through arctic snows

Possessed by a dream

That terrible to know

Treading, treading

Alien land

Where no man, by right

Should have strength to stand

But visions were mine

Hegira, crusade

'Til an ice cave became

My palisade

I looked down,

to find Quest done

A heap of golden skulls

Had I there won

And I played there

Among scintillant bone

Having come not to take

But to add my own.

(1988)

COUNTING COUP

It is said that

among certain North American

Indian tribes

the object in war was not to

kill the Other, but touch him

and escape, unharmed.

I understand the strategy.

There is no greater way

to hurt someone

than to touch him

and then

run away.

(1988)

THAT WHICH PERSEVERES

Why do I see

some leaves

—dry leaves, dead leaves—

still cling to the trees

even in winter gales,

when every winter

comes?

(1988)

CAT WITH FEATHERED TAIL

Cat with feathered tail,

You'll watch them drive

the nail, through this hand;

Yet Cat, understand

this Rock is not

your land.

(1988)

HAVAMAL

To strive

To carve

To write what

the world must

hear but cannot

see for lack

of one

good

Eye.

(1988)

UPON HIGH LANDS

Upon High Lands,

I prepare myself

a sacrifice.

"I don't get it. I mean

are you preparing a sacrifice

for someone? Or are you

the sacrifice? Or is the sacrifice

to you?"

You have said it. Is that not how

a man once proclaimed ...

"What? Proclaimed what …?

"I mean, I just don't get it."

(1992)

ICONS, & ICONOCLASTS

Icons, and iconoclasts.

Upon heather's tangled mass, in dreams

I waited. Painted. Tattooed.

Finding only old shield bosses,

spear heads. A few rusty iron fetters.

Your letters, when they came,

they came on other tongues.

Runes, forgotten

in translation now.,

Icons, and iconoclasts.

In wind and rain I'd stand until

ghosts of Latin soldiers passed, singing

in vino veritas. But eventually, too,

they'd pass, like water,

trickling down the hillside.

Me, just a Pict,

bearing your picture

scratched

in the back.

Icon, and me

struggling

to play

iconoclast.

(1992)

TOO EARLY, IN THE MOURNING

(And He cried out, in a loud voice,

    saying Eli, Eli, lama sabachthani,

    which means ...)

    Mourn

      mourn that

    which so

    long ago

    ceased

      to be a man for

it was Man

    but

    more,

      mourn for the Children.

(1992)

JESUS DREAMS, AND STRANGER THINGS

Dreams are the offerings

of many spiders

Spiders feed on flies.

***

"And there he was, in The Last

Temptation of Christ, saying,

'Do you know what I see when I

see an ant, when I look into its

shiny black eye ... I see the

face of God."

"Who? Jesus?"

"No, dummy—Willem Dafoe."

(1992)

ENOCH

Heat waves shimmer and distort visions in front of him. They turn the desert to dun-colored illusions.

There are no oases ...

His boots scuff across the grainy sand.

Water has come, has fled, has left the earth to dry. The ground is cracked into patterns that do not match. It is nature's form of tile floor. Perfect, fashionable tile for a perfect, fashionable four-bedroom rambler in a perfect, fashionable suburban cul-de-sac.

He has three layers of cotton socks. All are damp and make his feet itch. He needs the socks. He needs to prevent blisters from his heavy boots. He needs.

The boots. There are snakes in some places. He has heard this.

The buttes are towers of sienna and burnt umber rising from the floor of the desert. They were towers. They seem towers.

He thinks of dragons and kings.

Stories. Parables. They are only images, caused by desert heat.

Patches of dry grass grow more frequent. The boy looks to the horizon. Just over it the terrain varies even more. He knows this. He knows much.

He stops. He removes his olive-drab canvas backpack. He uses the pack as a backrest when he sits. The slightly rolling, dry fields are where he will set up his pup tent.

He reaches behind, unstraps one of three round canteens from the backpack. He drinks. The water is lukewarm. It is sweet. It hurts when he gulps too hard. The flesh inside his throat is dry and raw. But he thirsts.

He wets his palm, with it his cracked lips and the skin near his eyes. He sighs, and he coughs.

The boy's thin legs are sun-bronzed. The cutoff wool military pants offer no protection from the sun. The face is young and not yet angular. The hair is bleached now, by sun. The gaze is dull and too-aware. He has had German classes but does not know about angst. His feeling is unnamed.

He looks up. He sees a figure move slowly across the desert toward him from too far for the figure to have whispered and the boy to have heard. He hears the whisper retroactively. The stranger's gait is casual.

He has his hands in his pockets. His outline is distorted by the heat waves. His shoulders are broad, powerful, but the man seems incapable of harming anything. Or simply unwilling.

Aura, the boy thinks tangentially. But perhaps, he thinks, it is only the impression from the heat waves.

The man strides forward without blinking or averting his gaze. He comes close enough for his face to be visible. His hair is medium length. His beard is trimmed close to his face. The face is neutral. It does not yet smile, but seems to. It says hello.

The boy responds. He does not wish to avoid response, but could not hold it back even if he so wished. The distance between them is too close in the vastness of the desert. The stranger asks if he is going up to the buttes.

Yeah, the boy says. He guesses so.

The stranger's face does not change. An impression of a smile intensifies. The boy feels relieved. He has been told "yeah" is a bad word. One must only say "yes, sir." Especially when one does not mean it.

The stranger asks why. Why does the boy

go to the buttes? The boy shrugs. It was nice, being out there alone sometimes.

Alone, the man ponders out loud. Out here, there is not much else.

"It depends on what you know to look for."

The stranger's nonexistent smile widens. The boy feels the man's comment was a test and the boy has somehow responded correctly. The boy knows this is only a feeling. He knows he is an unnecessary romantic. Or, more correctly, he has been told he is a derogatory word meaning "unnecessary romantic."

"There's an eagle that nests on one of the buttes. I watch him sometimes.

"Want to walk over there with me? It's still early."

The boy starts setting up his tent a distance from the cliffs. The man watches. The boy says he needs some distance to see the eagle well. He can't see anything looking straight up. The man nods.

"You can see him too. Just wait." The boy brings out something swaddled in heavy padding. He unwraps it. He does so gently. It is Christmas season. He cannot afford the risk of breaking this thing. He is only allowed to ask for something during Christmas.

On Christmas Eve the boy goes to

church. He does well in Sunday School. Everyone there says he is such a good and smart and polite young man, but he knows they lie. If they did not they would not just tell these compliments but fight if need be to make them believed in the boy's house. But it was good that the church-people lied. If they did not, what kind of home would he have? It was so good that church-people lied, thought the boy, or he would have to admit that he had no home and be without it and soon starve, in the desert of the world.

He was in the desert now. He had often been here, and knew to find food. But this desert was only a game. He had been told that any desert he walked in was only a game.

He unswaddled his baby: a spotting scope, 5-30X, with zoom magnification. You can use it too, the boy says to the man. "Just be careful. I saved up summer work money a long time for this."

"How long?"

The boy shrugs. "Does it matter?"

"How long?" The man repeats so softly the boy can hardly hear him.

"Three years." The boy whispers back.

The man's sad eyes say that three years is a long
time for a boy. The boy shrugs.
He is used to it. The hard part was not the saving.
The hard part was having such a prize and having
to keep it hidden at a friend's house. The friend
was good but might still steal the scope, though the
boy shared it often.

If "the old man" had known of the scope he would
have broken it before the boy's eyes. His "old
man" is a priest. He is also an electrician but he
preaches of the value of a dollar. He harasses the
boy with chores so long as he is at home and is
angered at the boy's sometimes-habit of going off
without permission; he made the boy toil at the
local work farm each summer to pick string beans
and told him this was necessary employment for
the boy would amount to no better. The boy picked
beans in the autumn too, when he was ridiculed for
being no good in the sports he was not allowed to
play.

He should have been good at these games without
playing. He picked beans when he should have
been doing his work for school, but made top
grades anyway. This was good for had he not it
would confirm he "would amount to nothing." At
least he was not in the deserts, and starving.

Mother said nothing, or sometimes a little. The boy knew he had to be grateful. If he was not, they said, no one else would have him. No one but the desert.

All knew and hated the boy for getting top marks, for he was as a sissy and a nerd and a freak; all thought this, the old man sneered, did not the boy realize all thought this? No one at school said this but the boy knew him right. Despite their words of praise the church-people thought this.

However, the old man is equitable when he sneers at the boy for being "sensitive." It was not only men who are not supposed to cry. Women also. Women should not cry because they should not think big thoughts, or know anything but elation in his presence, and at the things he can buy them.

The old man has no daughters. It is better that way. Perhaps the old man would make a radical exception with daughters, but the boy does not know what good that would do.

The boy is not allowed nice things. He is not allowed nice things, even though the old man is "well off." The boy saved three years and three days for the scope. That he already understood how to work hard and be a man would not have pleased the old man, who is not really the boy's own "old man," and not so old anyway.

"I like your scope."

The boy shrugs. It is a common reaction of his.

He cannot keep the scope in his room. He cannot look on it with pride as he lies in bed and the lights wink out. The scope is not an object but a free and conscious friend. The boy does not consider it his. In this world, he possesses nothing. He has grown to like things this way.

The man walks from the camp. The boy is surprised. He follows to the foot of the pillar of rock. The man unslings his backpack. He removes rock-climbing gear: chock stones, nuts, karabiners, webbing, nylon rope.

The boy asks, You're going to climb the butte? The stranger nods. Alone? the boy asks. The stranger takes the circular piece of webbing and folds it into a diaper harness around his waist and legs. and connects the harness with a locking karabiner.

"Why?" the boy says.

The man shrugs. He starts to climb.

The boy returns to his camp. He positions his spotting scope to watch the man's progress. The man's advance is slow. He places very few anchors at the low points on the rock. The boy does not know if the man is reckless or conserving them for when the need is greater.

The boy repositions the spotting scope. He aims it to where the eagle's nest sits on a small ledge near the summit. He focuses. The bird is present. This is unusual. The eagle likes to soar on the updrafts at this time of day. It hunts. He is unsure what it hunts for.

Sometimes it just circles the butte.

The boy zooms in. The movement of the eagle's wings are wrong. The boy refocuses. One of the wings hangs at an odd angle.

The boy licks his lips. The eagle is too high. It cannot return to ground. The precision needed in the descent is too great.

It cannot descend. It cannot return. But the break is too large. It will not heal of its own accord.

With no other choice, the Great Bird of Prey might try and fall and crash, pained and delirious.

It is later. The climber moves up the rock. The boy sees him place each anchor. The man is halfway to the summit. It has taken until noon to get that far. His path will take him up through the ledge where the eagle roosts.

The boy wishes he could call up to the man. A wounded eagle might strike out. It might not comprehend that no harm was meant. Such a bird's talons could cause much damage. And this eagle can go nowhere. The man could easily avoid it if he so wishes.

The boy does not so wish. He does not want to warn the man. He hopes the man would come upon the bird. He wishes the man will save the bird. The boy knows it is unrealistic to hope. He knows he only hopes because he is an unnecessary romantic. Or a derogatory word that means "unnecessary romantic."

The eagle is clear in the lens of the scope. The wing is broken midway along its length. When the bird tries to move the limb the outer portion flops.

Dusk comes when the man is twenty yards from the summit. Darkness makes viewing through the spotting scope impossible.

The boy can see the man reach the ledge. The eagle will not take kindly to the intrusion. The boy expects commotion.

He looks. He sees none. He listens. He hears nothing. It means there is nothing. Sound carries far in the desert.

The moon happens to rise behind the butte. The boy sees the man and the eagle silhouetted. It does not lash out at him.

The boy does not sleep. He writes in his journal. He writes poems. He writes them in a notebook always kept hidden lest it be ripped before his eyes: the eyes of a sissy, and a nerd, and a freak.

The boy wakes. He sits up. The sun tops the butte. The brilliance sits upon the ledge. It blinds him. He still cannot see the man or the bird. The man will die. He has not come down. He has no water, the boy remembers. It has been three whole days, or perhaps four.

He must thirst, thinks the boy, for I do. I thirst.

The boy cannot wait much longer. He will be missed. He has left without permission. "The old man" will be angered. The old man does not care about the boy's welfare. But he has been gone without permission.

The boy walks north. When he goes a mile he can see the ledge. He sets up the spotting scope. Looking through it he sees neither bird nor man. He does see the man's climbing rope. It is just now cut loose, though the boy can see no one release the top end. It tumbles off the butte to the ground.

The boy scans the butte. Nothing living clings to the rock. He looks up from the scope. The eagle, circling off the butte, is a familiar shape. It flies strangely as if in pain.

It tries to soar. You cannot soar, the boy thinks, it is too late and your wing is broken. You will fall and you will die. The boy does not speak, however; not that the eagle could understand such speech. But the boy does not speak, for he understands that the eagle would die anyway, in the desert, in the nest. It merely would not fall.

The boy sees the eagle's wing buckle at the apex of the ascent. Momentum carries the shape into the glare of the sun.

The boy waits and watches, though the light burns his eyes. He waits for the bird to fall. It has to. He knows it has to. He has been told it has to.

The bird does not fall.

The boy waits for perhaps a half-hour but the heavens are silent. He wonders what to do. But he is still a boy, and this desert only a game.

He takes up his pack. He starts to return. He has been gone without permission. He will be punished.

MOVING DAY

Black, indifferent clouds

puff across the sun,

darken my face, and brows,

as I flip the latch,

pull back the lever, and

roll open the rear door.

Abused and withered,

parched and hungry,

my Muse hides in the back

of a U-Haul truck,

barely able to lift glazed eyes

as I approach,

saying nothing to Her.

Eventually She loses interest.

Ignores my timid, panting breath;

goes back to rifling through

the stack of small bills: a few

ones and fives—our meager

moving allowance.

(Such a generous company

we work for.)

She's forgotten what I can't.

That I once did it all for Her.

And I don't know what's worse;

don't know if I'd rather

have Her recall it all,

shrieking and hounding me

with reminders of all

my broken promises,

launching accusations at my face

with fire, and acid, and flying spit.

Or if I prefer this slow, delirious dream

that eats away at Her,

She never understanding

any reason for the

unstopped accumulation

of arthritic aches.

I still dream, too. Dream one day

I'll be able to put Her out

of that nagging misery;

pull the trigger, snap

tight the noose.

But I couldn't live without Her

in the beginning.

I can't live without Her

now.

And so I keep Her,

like a starving, sickly pet,

hoping someday, in desperation,

She'll show the strength

I always told myself

She had.

Peel back the steel skin

of Her cage,

lock her gaze on me,

and with flailing claws

and sharp teeth,

make a last meal.

Of our heart.

(2001)

BOUNDARY WATERS

There is this girl. A rock.

Languid, she swims

to the still urge.

Bare skin in the moaning

Void watches the Mother

Storm approach, to produce:

a whisper. Droplets,

in the liquid pool. Whorls,

from a breeze, in melted wax

on our cabin windowsill.

I see Triple,

and the faces of my goddesses cry,

as I pant my madness, focused

on the one lust that escapes

the grip of chanting, bitter,

ancient powers.

I, their Dionysus.

The ugly tongue of my Chorus

and theirs the same:

different in how melodious,

perhaps, but all our words

and phrases in my own first

language. Aching

blood finally dissipating

into more delicate waters.

Anima animated, and me.

Drunk on horse lather, and broth.

And my own raw

Shadow.

(2001)

BILDUNGS ROMAN

In her, bare rust,

and lust, is a gift,

and a vision.

Of a gorgeous honey-woman,

who drives a summer shadow

under a rocky moon.

And by languid, luscious mist

a goddess from the purple waters,

spring wind and our

delicate sleep, is sad, as mad,

milky Death.

An ache in a beating sea,

like the chant of foaming lather,

or the iron love

polished by whispers,

put to one, raw

light.

Illumination

for the operation.

Life's knife

manipulating the Void

into an elaborate,

giant

Lie.

(2001)

BIOS (Basic Input Output System) v.5.5

The oldest recorded survivor of a prostratotomy in relief of hypognostimanic impotitus, Robert Subiaga, Jr. now lives happily in a place not too far from Wisconsin, the home of beer, cheese, and serial killers.

There, Bob spends his time in the cattle-barn, catching mice, rats and other small rodents and batting them around before eating them.

At least when he's not writing advertising copy for God.

Neither Bob nor God is allowed on the furniture though. That's for company.

THE YEAR WE MADE CONTACT

Hot, humid—a bad day to wait for a bus in Minneapolis. When I first saw her what I noticed was how sweat trickled under her Lycra tank-top, with a "Batman" logo threatened by darkness spreading between her breasts. Clear there was nothing underneath the T.

I thought she should've worn a bikini top, or a bra. An understated lace bra to go with her skirt and Doc Martens and no-lens tortoise-shells would've been fashionable. Hard for Lyn-Lake's hipsters to keep up with Bed-Stuy these days. Her bag was big, but not heavy, and she had that swagger. The one of an independent woman, not entirely secure in her independence. But then again, whoever was?

I pulled my red Corvette up next to her. Song blaring by our local hero, The-Artist-Formerly-Known-As-&-Now-Again-What's-His-Name. Not coincidentally, *Little Red Corvette.*

No intention to say anything to her. Just enjoying the afternoon, and the thought I could have said something.

"'Sweatin' to the Oldies today?" she called out.

Then stared at me like a woman about to fend off a shark when I looked back. Like a woman used to it. Is that what I was? Or at least how I looked?

I'm sure I did. Well over two decades on her. I tried an innocent smile. Nodded to the stereo and said "Coincidence. Think I planned this?"

"No," she said. Then, "Think I did."

Cheeky girl. I blushed. Turned the music off.

"So that's you trying to assert free will?" she chuckled. "Pathetic."

I looked sheepishly straight ahead, waiting for the traffic signal to change.

"Offer me a ride," she ordered.

"Would you like a ride?" I obeyed. How had she …?

It must have been in her eyes. …Nice eyes. *Hazel? Blue? What **was** that color?*

She suddenly hopped in the passenger side. Smiled. Said something I didn't catch as I looked straight down and tried to avoid that gaze. I didn't even recall touching the stereo knob again, even as the speakers came to life.

1999.

"S'OK," she just about snarled hungrily. "I like the Oldies."

"Good," I said. "As I am one." And remembered when I first heard that song, in high school. Just as I remembered when the day came and 1999 spilled over into a second millennium and even from something as trite as two or four digits for a year code like two or three fingers to make the sign of the cross in Old Russia it didn't really matter after all and the world didn't end.

Yet. In the end, of course, it always does. Entropy wins, in the end. Even over Them.

As if she could read my mind, or at least my face, this thought seemed to touch her. A hand that felt like something too cool to be skin came to rest lightly on my arm and I chanced a look at her again out of the corner of my eye, honestly fearing either the possibility this wasn't flesh or that it was.

"So… Where you from?" Stupid question.

"Stupid." She confirmed. "Ask where I'm going," she commanded.

"Where are you going," I said. My tongue was starting to go numb.

"Anywhere I want." This came more kindly. But, sometimes, kindness can mean only more pain is coming.

Then she pointed an elegant finger that could have been freckled and not scaled, if freckles were sea-green, her too-long and too-slender tongue peeking out to lick too-wet and too-pink lips, and run over too-sharp teeth.

Scolding me, "Hey, pay attention. The light's green."

BIOS (Basic Input Output System) v.6.6

Robert Subiaga, Jr. prefers to remain an enigma.

As with most of his aspirations, however, he expects this one to be crushed by Fate's cruel design.

WILDERNESS

The horse was of a cross incorporating much of an Old English Black Horse and an Arabian. For speed. For power. Most of all, for wildness. Its heavy hooves pawed the thick fluffs of shallow, fresh snows into small, quicksilver sprays, but under that the harder pack of the glacier was more treacherous than it appeared as the horse and rider descended into the surer footing of the valley.

The snow from the moving hooves caught, then diffracted, the reddening sunset, and the horse snorted its breath in equally frosty clouds.

Whenever these vapors dispersed just as fast, they revealed the rider even more clearly. Seen from below, limned by the sun, the beast and man together would have seemed one, a centaur, both covered in furs and steel and leather. Armor against the monster that could be the cold. Armored against other threats as well.

The horseman's one good eye squinted impassively, the other covered by a brown leather patch. When he pulled away his scarf and face mask his weathered face scowled like a masque, even more so for his frosted black goatee, as he sat straight in the saddle and reined and the horse, be it nervous or excited or both, paced.

With mechanical precision the man turned his head; went from scanning the drifts in the white-and-grey distance to watching those at the horse's hooves. He suddenly dismounted, clearly having found something of interest, his scabbarded weapons clinking, his leather-encased armor creaking.

That one good eye glimmered, iron-grey and unreflecting. Its iris mirrored the overcast sky's diffuse brightness no differently than did the battered steel of the horned and visored bascinet helmet that hung from the saddle like a grinning metal skull.

 He knelt. One gloved hand dug at a dark protrusion in the snow. A small object surfaced from the deeper, harder crusts, carved of dark wood that nearly had petrified to a reflective black.

A Celtic cross. Except this one had not a single crossbar, but a doubled one, both crossing the main stave and intersecting each other in an X-shape. And to this one was crucified a bald, wedge-headed figure, with four arms to correspond with, and be nailed to, the X crossbars.

It would have been strange enough that Celtic crosses of this type rarely took the form of a crucifix. To add to this the mutant shape was almost comical, though the agony of the crucified figure was unquestionably serious.

The horseman allowed himself a wry smile. To only him, and select few others, this cross was no joke. It identified a very specific, esoteric order.

Lodinian, he thought. The rare icon of one of the followers of the barely known Kargin Lodin.

The horsemen's face shared nothing of his other thoughts, if he entertained any, while he scanned the surrounding drifts.

He picked one whose shape was not wavy and crested but dull, wide, irregular. He moved toward it. The artifact was still held loosely in one hand. With the other he began to clear snow away from the drift.

A few inches deep he encountered a forearm; its owner had frozen while reaching upward, even dying of exposure, almost as if the last act of a dedicated supplicant.

The horseman saw traces of a crude, homespun garment, clinging to hardened flesh and icy skin. The dead man's hand itself had no gloves, no mittens, even in the harshness of this wilderness.

It made sense; the Lodinians were a crude cult more or less within the Franciscan orbit. The curiosity was that they had adopted a crucified form of their saint to venerate when Lodin had died—according to all of the few accounts—in the throes of either divine revelation or syphilitic convulsion. Yet, like all Franciscans they maintained a vow of poverty.

They would have preached against protection of gloves or mittens as frivolous, connotative of easy living, and materialism.

The horseman shrugged. Neither spirituality, nor outright mysticism, nor any descending avatar of their version of any man-god, be it Yeshua or Lodin or some synthesis, had saved this pilgrim from the simple vicissitudes of cold, and entropy.

If there was salvation anywhere, the horseman thought as he winced, and half-doubled over. The pain in his side was sharp, but transient. It passed. He had become used to its unexpected visits. He did not let it worry him. He would not likely die yet. Not today.

He returned to his horse, palmed the religious artifact. There would be enough representatives of the Church convening in the area shortly. On the massive keep would they converge: a fortress of single structure excavated from the snows of the mountain *Cous*, on the icecap glacier *Vatnajokull*, on the edge of the great glacial-volcanic lake there.

The horseman judged the body he had found to be quite old, preserved by the cold on this peak, which was part of the smaller glacier *Tindfjalljokull*. "Smaller" was, of course, a relative value judgment. As with all glaciers, the ice here never melted.

This island that the Norse settlers called *Island*, or Ice-Land, others, as few and obscure as the Lodinians, called *Chicgroen*. It supposedly meant "once green" in a bastard marriage of Old Norse and a tidbit remainder of a far older, perhaps Pictish, tongue.

Again, supposedly. There had been monks, by some accounts Irish, in any case Celtic, on Iceland when the Norse settlers had arrived.

Just as any earlier pilgrims, though, these most recent ones would have what the horseman thought of as no realistic idea of what it was they really sought. Peace? Heaven? Oneness?

And yet would be dogged in that quest.

There were words; carven, linear gouges in an archaic, non-Norse runic tongue, on the back of the cross. But ones the horseman had learned, in his many travels, to read.

God is Love.

He pocketed the relic. Mounted up, framed in the iron sky.

What happened when Love was tainted? What happened when Love died?

What happened when Love became monstrous, by simple fact that it could *not* die?

He sat for a time and pondered this. And did not spur his great horse toward the next valley, until the sun had begun to set.

– from *The Gnostic*

11/11

Sun. Wind. Wave.

Let it lie. Use all these days,

To hurry out from my Fall,

drop like leaves; go

with this early need.

A summer fling. A moment

for remembering, that

one warm, red balm

can dance through the sky,

light as a curve,

long and gentle,

and after dark

still be

a cold rain over

empty, winter morning

shadows. But bless you,

you chill, stormy moon.

Weekly surrender.

Ask her, "Why?"

Was she ever

your dream friend,

gold child,

Green Mother?

Then listen how

what love hears

will not sleep:

an open breath

like vanished snow

even presently

to wander the Earth,

murmuring blue

songs, come

every spring.

(2001)

ODD MAN OUT

Were he less

odd, should blowy Time

really march about:

march, as a sudden star,

here, there,

throw it All off?

Dare.

Dare shape,

share

the deeper,

Ram-fathered hours?

See me.

See me tell him:

turn,

feel,

begin

the Year.

(2001)

FATHER BE

I'll tell her

let me fill you.

She is there,

as soon as these long, curved shadows

of twilight, like odd dancers, begin to fling

themselves about, until needing

their own sudden surrender.

Were she a sleepy, blue song,

seeking the boy,

his breath would instead wander,

eventually through a spring rain,

a fall wave, even the wintergreen

hue of stormy, summer skies.

Until, frustrated,

she finally realizes

this burst dam, will bless not

her love, but leave her winded,

as if from all use, and

blown out with the new snow

before it can ever melt to fill

her basins.

Weeks, again, come and go.

I tell you, feel

the dropless Earth lie

at rest. Seek the Man.

And when you ask yourself,

How can he see me off

on my voyage? I'll tell you,

Hurry, and let's throw off

the long, hourly moment.

Be, sweet listener, like the cold day's

sunlight: a red chill, that can march

to any horizon, can turn to gold

my long-vanished mornings.

I'll tell your friend to tell you: Come

to remember the Open Deep,

after what timely dark there was

your ever-present moon mother.

And me.

Where I hope

to overhear you

ask an early, gentle dream

from your first consciousness

for one glimpse of that one star,

murmuring my warm balm:

Father be here, child,

why are you

empty?

Be no more

Empty.

(2001)

WOLVES TALES, 2

If you perhaps thought we were finished with our tales of the North Woods, rest assured: we are not. Though much time did pass without great event. Nearly two centuries. Why that is, especially since the cycles of the moon are certainly monthly, no one knows.

But such it was. Perhaps there was the need for woods to have grown over from where neither native nor settler have been for too long a time. Perhaps mother Earth needed to endure enough transgressions from those who would ravage her. Perhaps, her more savage face merely needed the proper prey.

In any case, in time, the North Woods became prime timber country. Prime, once again virgin timber, perfect in the eyes of a rapacious lumber baron. And his company indeed moved in, and for a decade he grew rich and powerful off harvesting the bodies of the trees.

But after that decade, the forest quiet in response to her loss, came the start again, of the disappearances.

Now it came from the lumber camp, and the victims were the occasional lumberjack. As the legend of the Voyageurs described, so it was with each lumberjack going missing. Here and there, though often enough just within earshot of his comrades, a lumberjack, no matter how young or strong or sometimes in that moment sober, would be suddenly gone, with nothing to mark his passing but perhaps a few drag marks through the forest floor, at most a drop or two of blood.

The misty legend of the child monster from centuries before was well known to the lumberjacks, but now they started referencing it more often, first in mostly joking tones, but soon enough in more serious ones.

But the lumber baron, the Boss, would have none of it. He hired first one hunter, then another, then a third. All experienced at the elimination of wolves, as well as bears, cougars—even a few of the great lions or tigers or crocodiles of far off continents.

Yet each hunter soon enough went missing as well. As if whatever or whoever preyed upon them knew to target them first.

The Boss was near apoplectic in rage, his lumberjacks starting to desert him, when a terrifying figure showed up at the lumber baron's mansion. Draped in a multitude of impossible large wolf pelts, fringed leather and wide-brimmed hat, this fourth hunter had a deeply scarred face. At his side was a lever action carbine and a pair of revolvers in worn holsters—and in the loops of the belt and bandolero, cartridges whose tips gleamed, silver cores inserted into the drilled-out noses of the lead bullets.

The Boss snarled at the hunter asking what kind of costume this was, and the hunter replied in kind that the Boss already knew. This hunter was not a wolf hunter—no, nor one of bears or even tigers. He was a werewolf hunter, and the world's foremost one—if perhaps only currently surviving one—at that. And the Boss needed his services.

Reluctantly, sneering at this newcomer, the Boss nevertheless agreed to pay the man his weight—in silver—if he were to rid the lumber camps of this menace.

The werewolf hunter soon had set up his operation near the main camp: a tree stand outside the longhouses where the lumberjacks were bunked. And from which the last man had disappeared, having been unable to resist going out in the middle of the night to urinate. For a time men had been disappearing intermittently from near the outhouses, so that the tactic had changed to sneak out near the cabins proper, but the last man to be lost had been plucked from right under the cabin windows beside which his comrades had slept.

In the earliest hours of the morning, a lumberjack emerged, groggy-eyed but terrified at the same time. And as he started to micturate, the werewolf hunter indeed saw an incredibly large but dark figure move through the woods toward him, massive as a grizzly but shambling swiftly on two canine rear legs.

With perfect aim honed by years of experience, the werewolf hunter drew down and fired, right through where the Beast's heart should be. And, instantly, it dropped.

The werewolf hunter descended, pointed to the shocked and trembling lumberjack and then toward the longhouse, and motioned the man back inside.

Then, soon enough, another large lupine pelt had been stripped and staked out for tanning, to soon add one more cloak to those in the werewolf hunter's storage chests.

You might think the tale would then be over *now*. In which case, again, you would think wrong.

One week later, the werewolf hunter was summoned to the mansion of the Boss. And not only was his silver payment not waiting, there stood the contingent of the US Cavalry and the local sheriff. Letting the werewolf hunter know in no uncertain terms that not only had he not completed his task—the entire contingent of lumberjacks in the employ of the Boss in the North Woods was dead. The whole assembly of longhouses had been turned into an abattoir, dead men everywhere.

The Cavalry commander made it clear the alleged werewolf hunter could not be personally responsible, that indeed would have strained credulity. Yet he was under suspicion of colluding with Indian tribes—though none existed for hundreds of miles around—and should the new lumberjacks being brought in for employment be lost, a single one of them, the werewolf hunter would be arrested and hanged.

His teeth gritted, the werewolf hunter returned to the camp, and set up in the night in a new tree stand. As the full moon rose over the very early morning, the hunter watched—and saw a familiar large shape move through the woods toward the longhouses.

The werewolf hunter drew aim and fired, and the massive shadow dropped. But then, to the hunter's shock, rose unsteadily. Stretched itself. And started loping toward the cabins again.

A second shot dropped it again, but it rose again; then a third shot barely made it stumble. Then, making hackles rise on the werewolf hunter's neck, he saw a second shadow moving through the woods, and a third. Soon enough, a full dozen lupine shapes—at least as many lycanthropes as the hunter had ever skinned—were converging on the longhouses.

The werewolf hunter started to scramble down the tree, but by the time he was to the forest floor the shadows were rampaging through the longhouse and cabins, men screaming and blood spattering against the windows and out the doors.

Finally, dark shapes started to spill back out from the cabins, their crimson, glowing eyes turning to fix on the hunter. He fired one shot, then another, then another into the approaching mass, but the effect barely registered.

Turning, the werewolf hunter started to flee— seeing the only place of refuge was the storehouse to the chow hall. He rushed inside, breaking the outer lock with the butt of his carbine and throwing himself inside, then dropping the wooden bar across the inner part of the door to bar it from the inside. Checking his revolvers, he steeled himself and waited, seeing the first of dawn light creeping over the horizon through a small window. If the thick door and walls could hold for even a minute he had a chance.

But as the monstrous snouts started to mist right through the heavy wood, only to resolidify on the other side, and emptying his revolvers' chambers slowed the attackers not in the least, a curious realization was the last thought the werewolf hunter knew.

Silver might be bane to werewolves indeed. But, clearly, meant nothing to a werewolf's *ghost*.

BROKEN SYMMETRY

The poet sees

a homeless man.

The homeless man

sees the poet.

The mirror cracks.

The mirror

breaks.

(2001)

LEFT, WITH THE WAITER

Turning and turning in the widening gyre: The
falcon cannot hear the falconer

"And in short, I was afraid."

For a moment there seemed respite.

Me Pacific, at the edge

of losing consciousness

to the beat of pattering

rain music

smoothed into strings,

wood winds,

tiptoe percussions.

Little feet. Spirits of

that which should have been

conceived, in our listening.

But mountains do not move,

and Muhammed has come here:

"We all Dream, and when we wake

we die."

Here, I wonder, now,

are all my conceptions

of future, stillborn?

Conceptions of past,

aborted?

I feel only

an empty Present.

Open my eyes

to a Night that is

perfectly clear.

And black.

Nothing to do to be heard

even self to self.

Nothing to do but crack a fifth

(strain an octave)

down it all in the silence

of about half an hour.

As, quiet, comes

Apocalypse.

(bang and whimper, one)

But You are not

here.

And I forever

wait.

(2001)

CAFÉ NIRVANA

Eight cups of coffee, is just the right amount,

to get a concentration in the blood

that is more than trivial,

and less than lethal.

But it's a different matter to take it further.

Dance, on the edge.

The death caused by a stimulant overdose

is interesting to behold: shakes,

and heart palpitations: beats

that tick along so fast

that heart has no time

to fill,

and the effect is the same as if it doesn't

... even ... squeeze,

at all.

I'm sure there are spastic visions

of the same kind, in the same moment.

Visions that dance so fast

just beyond your fluttering eyelids,

that if you could ask the dying one,

I mean, if they could come back

for just a moment, from the brink,

and just a little beyond,

their dreams would be

blind.

Pointless tremors. All sound

and fury, and

empty.

I've always been partial to trinities.

I'll take a third triple-shot, please.

It's a tough route to nirvana,

but if my conscience tries to bother me

about it, all it has to do is

Make something of it.

(2001)

BLASPHEMING

One cannot *sacre*

    who would not

profane.

One cannot prophecy

    who would not

blaspheme.

And One cannot love

    what he would never

kill.

           (1993)

THE WEEPING DRAGON

There is a tale of a Great Dragon, who lives among a settlement of elfin people. And forever weeps.

There once was a dragon. But He was not like the legends described dragons. He did not eat elfin people, or burn them with fire, or spit acid on them, or step all over their houses.

And the dragon came upon a surprise. If elfin peoples were allowed to grow old, and not be burned, or stepped all over, or spit upon, some of them became dragons themselves.

They were not all like him; some had no wings, some could not breathe fire but only spit acid, or lightning, or even merely spittle. But all had one thing in common: they also did not thoughtlessly burn or eat elfin babies, or children, or step all over their houses, or spit upon them.

And all other dragons watched over the elfin peoples, though none more than the first dragon.

And, in time, all these other dragons went on, in search of other worlds, and other elfin peoples to watch over, that they might one day be dragons themselves, someday.

And it came to pass that the first dragon realized that, although he watched over them, the elfin people still were wary of him, and feared him.

And the first, greatest dragon gathered all the elfin peoples together and said, "You have no need to fear me. See, I pull aside the scales of my breast, and whoever would strike a blow may do so. I am your protector, and defender, and shall always bare my whole and vulnerable heart to you."

And none of the elfin people struck him with their elfin swords, and the dragon was glad.   But he did not know that the elfin people had each murmured to himself, or herself, and to each other this thought: "If we struck, but did not at once destroy this dragon, his rage might be fierce, so we had best not strike at all."

And so one day the dragon said, "I must walk together with these elfin people, for I know that though they accept me and would not harm me, yet do they fear me."

And the dragon called upon the magic of the Creators, Sky and Earth, and all the Others, and they granted him to walk among the elfin people as a human, though They insisted he not be quite so small as they, but tall and proud.

And the dragon walked among them.

And as he walked, he did not hear the elfin people each say to himself, or herself, and to each other, "This dragon is more a threat to us than ever. Before, as our protector and defender we could tolerate the threat of his power.

But now he is one of us, and even now as one of us is of no special use to us, and he is weak. But in his weakness still is the potential for strength, for he could yet become again a dragon among us, and be as we know dragons really are, and eat us, and burn us, and step all over our houses."

And together they thought, "Yet if we strike now, unlike before, we may even with our tiny, elfin swords eviscerate him with one blow, and split his heart, and he may die, and we need never again fear *any* dragons!"

And the elfin people said to the once-dragon, "Do you remember how you used to pull apart your breast scales and bare yourself to a blow, and say, Whoever would strike a blow may do so, I am your protector and defender and shall always bare my whole and vulnerable heart to you?' Would you show us once again, for old times' sake?"

And the dragon spread his arms and began to speak. But before he had finished the first words, the elfin people fell upon him, and tried in vain to eviscerate him with their tiny swords, and in vain to with their elfin swords split his great heart.

And the dragon stood for a moment, surprised, for even as a man their tiny, elfin swords could scarcely make so large a heart as his bleed, and could not kill him. But the once-dragon realized what they had meant to do to him, and from within his heart broke, and burst. And he fell.

And suddenly the sky split with lightning, and dripped with acid, and even merely spittle ...

... And hundreds of dark forms descended upon the elfin people, the many forms with wings carrying those without.

And the dragons surrounded the elfin people and said: "You fools! You nest of vipers! We have searched long and hard, yet have still not found any other elfin peoples. Did you not know that we would have watched over you, that some of you might grow into dragons yourself one day? And none more so than he, who you have killed!"

And the many dragons snatched the spirit of the First Dragon as it fled his body, and they returned to it its dragon power, and each living dragon infused it with a little of their own.

And the slain dragon rose, and his body changed into a dragon once again, more powerful and fearsome than any dragon had ever been.

And in their anger the dragons said: "These fools! This nest of vipers! Come, what matter is it that some would be dragons? Let us burn them *all*, and eat them *all*, and step all over *all* their houses!"

But the once and now-again Great Dragon said, *No. For there are those among them who will yet be dragons themselves, one day ...*

"Go," he said. "Find your own elfin peoples, while I watch over these. Though never again may I bare my whole heart to them."

And the Great Dragon lives among them, and watches over them still, and now, and in all ways.

Even unto the end of the World.

BIOS (Basic Input Output System) v.6.66

Robert Subiaga, Jr. is a local writer and teacher, and the smartest human being who has ever lived.

That is, next to the person who can prove why.

MAKING UP

I'm making this up as I go.

I swear I am.

Don't be fooled by appearances.

Don't be fooled by me appearing

to read off a page.

I didn't write this out.

I didn't plan this out

before I came to stand before you.

This Scripture, this credo, this revelation

is totally impromptu, is an enigma,

wrapped in a riddle, tossed in

a white, free, Protestant maelstrom.

Torn, between Scylla and Charybdis.

Torn—it solves the dilemma

nicely, doesn't it? Gets it over with?

The real pain, the pain of choosing

one's own demise, gets to disappear.

Seems to disappear.

I'm making this up as I go.

I swear I am.

Don't be fooled by appearances.

Don't be fooled by my quotes,

things attributed to me

that you might find later,

on a scrap of paper.

Correlation does not imply causation.

It's all your imagination. As if

I'm reading it off a page, as if

I thought it out

ahead of Time.

I am making this up as I go.

I swear I am.

And unraveling it all just as fast.

Unraveling everything.

Except for you.

(2001)

SUNDOWN, AT GORDIUM

I want to know

Naught but that:

Was the psychonaut's

Solution

to the psycho knot

Psycho

—or not?

(2001)

ANGEL, IN ORION

You shot into the field. My hunter.

You shot blind.

There was a Stag in the field, at night.

At night there was always a Stag in the field. Only at night.

And on a given night you might fire a hundred arrows, or a hundred thousand. Then you would search.

Sometimes you would search by sunlight, come the dawn. Sometimes you would search by lantern light, still in the dark.

And you would be lucky to find one arrow of your hundred, or hundred thousand.

"This is foolish," the ones who stood and watched, the ones who always stood and watched, the ones who only stood and watched, always said.

"You waste time. You waste arrows. You waste them, loosing blind in a field at night."

"You cannot hunt the Stag," said One, "For long before your arrows have come It will have fled. It is only there for those who do not look."

"You cannot hunt the Stag," said Another. "For your arrows cannot pierce the flesh of what is not flesh."

"You cannot hunt the Stag," said the Third. "For even to look upon Him is surely to be destroyed."

"You waste time," said All, "you waste arrows. You waste them, loosing blind into a field, at night."

Then, once in a while, on a given night, you would hit the Stag.

You make camp where it had fallen, and make fire. And you would skin it, and cook it; and you would rise, and eat.

"That must not be the Stag we meant," the ones who stood and watched, the ones who always stood and watched, the ones who only stood and watched, always said.

But you ate. They hungered. And I watched.

(2001)

BEAUTY (OR WOLVES TALES, 3)

Once there was a young woman, who would be a Princess, who would be a Queen.

And in her village there was a beautiful young man that she loved. And she wished to marry him, for he was young and strong and as a prince among the members of the small village, but was not a Prince among the world, for he had no great fortune.

And the beauty went out into the thick woods, where there was rumored to live a Great and Terrible Beast, in a castle gilded from base to summit, with a crystal palace within, and the Beast went about all day in the finest jackets and hose, roaring to the hot sun and the night stars.

But the young lady was sore afraid, for it was said that the Beast would kill all those who stepped into the thick woods.

And the Beast came upon her, and did no harm.
And he invited her to his Golden Castle, and his
Crystal Palace, in the Thick Woods. And the
beauty went with him, for she thought to herself:
"This Beast is fearsome, and most certainly savage
and untrustworthy, yet he has great gold and
fortunes, and I may be able to convince him to
give these to my love that he may be a Prince, and
I his Princess, and his Queen."

And the beauty dined with Beast. And at his table
were many four-footed animals of the earth, wild
creatures, reptiles, and fowl of the air. And before
the beauty's eyes they loved, and laughed, and
played, and fought, and devoured each other, and
were reborn.

And the beauty said, how is it you have these to
dine with you? And the Beast said: "These are my
charges, for I have been cursed by a Great Witch
and I am watcher of these woods, and whoever so
comes into these woods and will not live as a
charge must perish by my hand."

And the beauty said, "But are these not four-footed
beasts of the earth, wild creatures, reptiles, and
fowl of the air? And why would one, perhaps one
young and strong and as a prince among the

members of his village, allow himself to be your charge, and fight and play among these, and devour them, who are so known to be common, and unclean?"

And the beauty was sore afraid, for it was known that the Beast's rage was fierce. But the Beast was calm, and he spoke quietly, and said, "But you are not of my charges, and not my love, and I shall not harm you, but now must you leave."

And beauty was sore afraid, for it was known that the Beast's rage was terrible. And she moved to leave the Table, and the Golden Castle, and the Crystal Palace, and the horrible Beast.

And as she left she saw the Beast among his charges, in the thick woods. And she saw him among his charges, and all loved him,

And the beauty's said to herself, This Beast has said that he has been cursed by a Great Witch, and he lives in a Golden Castle, with a Crystal Palace, and wears the finest hose. Why, such a Beast must once have been a man, and a Prince, and I will love such a man, and be his Princess, and his Queen!

And she went into the thick woods, and spoke these words to Beast. And Beast turned away from her. And when the beauty asked why, he said: "You must cover your eyes, now, for my first curse is now to be lifted, by your words . . ."

And beauty closed and covered her eyes, and there was a great flash, as of lightning. And when she opened them, there stood yet a Beast, but the gilded castle was gone, as was the crystal palace, and the Beast's fine jacket, and hose, and all the palace's gold. "Now you see me as I am," the Beast said, "For not only am I and shall I ever remain a Beast, but I also have no fortune."

And the beauty turned away from him. "Then I will not have you," she said. And she ran away sad, for she expected much ...

***

And on the third day afterward, the Beast felt someone trespass in his woods. And he went out to find the intruder, and accept them as one of his charges or to cause him to perish.

And to the Beast's surprise, before him stood the beauty, her arms heavy with baskets of fruit for him.

"I cannot turn away from you," she said. "For I have seen how you love your charges, and how you tend these woods. And though you are Beast yet are you more lovely than any man, and though if you have me you may have no gold, you have great fortune. I love you, and will be forever with you, and if the witch who cursed you returns, I will fight her, though she make me like you, and cursed, and a she-Beast."

And the sky split with lightning, and the voice of the Great Witch descended. "Hear me," She said, "I am the Most High, and have made all things in my sight, and in my sight have I made all things good. And nothing that I have cleansed shall be called common, or unclean.

You have chosen well, Beauty, for although your love shall always be Beast, and always without gold or fortune, I shall give to you fortune that you may share with him, and entrust the Golden Castle and Crystal Palace to you that he may live with you, and you may aid him as he watches these woods, and protects his charges. And they shall be your charges always, and you will be their Beauty, and their Princess, and their Queen."

And Beauty and the Beast lived in the thick woods, among their charges, who laughed and played and *fucked* and hunted and fought and killed, and were born, and laughed, but always loved. And sometimes were they sad. But they lived happily ever after.

For as long as there ever could be an after.

AUTOSCOPY

I sometimes make the mistake of staring at the
neon lights of the city, out the window of the motel
room. I thought renting one would help. I thought
the cheaper the better. No go.

Usually I'd be working more in peace, taking in
the more welcome illumination of the full moon,
outside the window of the luxurious study my
habits have managed to pay for. Inspired, still,
after all the years. Glancing at the clock from time
to time instead of the neon, noting as it goes from
that Wow of 2 A.M. steadily toward 3:33. Always
having worked best at night.

I sit up, and my back creaks like the protesting
hardwood of that gothic mansion's floors, back
where I usually call home. But it's not like I
should be unused to being away from it either. Not
when I've spent so many nights in a dorm room on
campus too. Maintaining the façade.

I twirl my new-old (fresh bought antique)
fountain-pen between my long fingers again.
Another affectation, that I've tried to no avail.
(The pen that is. Not the fingers.) Before that was

the manual typewriter, even if I couldn't stand to use it in a hipster coffeehouse. Still, nothing breaking the routine seems to help any better than keeping the routine did earlier.

My head aches, and it is from nothing more, nor less, than the intensity of aborted thoughts.

He leans over the pockmarked oak desk and puts pen to paper. The words, still, for the first time, do not come. Will not come.

I contemplate opening the window to let in bittersweet scents that only a dirty city can give. Unlike many, at times I love the scents of ozone, and combustion exhaust, and even the faint whiff of street urine.

Her words echo. *Her* words, but not mine, for mine will not come in reply. *And this is the first time.* **This has never happened to me before ...**

I shake my head. No, no going for innuendo. Though it is funny now that, somehow, I even lust for her now. Though I wonder if thoughts of sex are just another insidious temptation to procrastinate.

Think of it as part of the assignment, I hear what she might say.

Describe, then? Well, my sexuality is, as they like to say, "alternative." Still, I lust for you, and wonder what it would be to take you. Effete and genteel, I wonder about having you in a way both eternal in character and yet violently consummated in its realization. How's that? Cozy, in a pagan and fleeting way?

 The rubber Halloween masks I have in the room—a werewolf—calls down from a shelf. I've had it since fall quarter of freshman year, an inspiration. A good-luck charm. That's when I first started selling big. But what is a mask?

I always thought I took as much joy in their destruction as their making, or using. But one has trapped me now. *The Invisible Man?*

I pick up my old muzzle-loading revolver. Brought it too. Genuine antique, I've had it forever.

I fiddle with it, wipe it with a cloth that glides over the clean oil on the metal. The last time I fired the revolver thunder roared and lightning laced from the painstakingly hand-loaded chambers and muzzle. Yet it was not only gunpowder that drove the flight of the projectile. The gun was a mere talisman. The real power came from me.

Once I shot a squirrel with it.

It looked like a small rodent, too small even to roast or stew, but it champed its teeth uselessly, until blood stopped spilling from its lips and soaking into the ground. Fitting sacrifice for a chthonic, hungry Mother. Oh, Nature is rarely so depicted, in her devouring form. But I've made my living from the fact that that repression needs an outlet.

I once read a nutritionist's article claiming humans were meant to be vegetarians because their first impulse on seeing an animal was to watch it, not pounce on it and tear it open with their teeth. Yet most humans have canines. Even those with dentures mimic having them.

I place the gun back on the desk. It is, of course, unloaded. The motel rules forbid firearms, and though I'll blithely break them it's a concession to hospitality that I'll keep it free of ammunition. I am nothing if ... uncivilized.

Good. You're opening up. Tell me more about yourself.

 What? That I've thought of using the gun on myself?

Have you?

I can't. And besides, it has no ammunition, remember?

Remember. Back in my secret study, I hear my Confederate Civil War saber calls vainly to me. Did you know that it still has stained flecks of Union blood? I was there, you know. There, and so many other places, and times. Lived, so many lives.

Interesting, she says. And it sounds like therapy.

All goes with my job, I say.

But she won't draw me out. Not any further.

 Not to ask what "really there" even means. What the distinction—if they are not in fact just a spectrum whose colors bleed into each other—is between what one thinks and what "is." What one imagines, and what is.

I sojourn to the bathroom, to "brush the old fangs," slap deodorant on, well, the old Pits. Then return to the desk, hoping I have a second wind.

Yet as soon as I grip the pen I struggle, hands trembling. Possessed. (Or perhaps more accurately not, as the case may be.)

Worse, I know any magick here is both more mundane and more powerful than any occult thing.

Horror so often is, I know. A hundred tales and forty novels bear my mark to attest to that. My mark, but not my name.

Pseudonymous all. I'd caught the genre on an upswing and helped fill the craving for the darkest of the lot. An old high school English instructor had somehow connected me with an agent with a reputation for six-figure deals, and then left education for that agency himself to ride my gravy train and make them seven.

Yet in a dual life, I still decided to pursue undergraduate work through part-time classes. It has taken eight years, but I will earn a degree. Pre-med. You'd expect surgery, I say to her, but I'm thinking more psychiatry.

If...

One more class to go. "Yours," I say to her. Three credits.

One that, almost giggling with the layers of deception behind it all, I'd thought: why not take Introductory Creative Writing?

Should have been an easy A.

Should have been. Life is full of them. *Should-have-beens.*

I rush across the bedroom to the bathroom again, nauseous, leaning over the sink and vanity. *Just write a character sketch*, she had said.

No problem. I've done a thousand of them,

Easier yet. Everyone, do a character sketch of yourself.

Yourself.

"Yes. You know, describe yourself. You background. Your history. Mentally, emotionally..."

Physically.

I look up for the hundredth time tonight. Pleading into the dirty, streaked mirror.

Pleading. If only there were a reflection.

URCHIN

The little girl, she begged me, "don't."

And then I knew I couldn't leave.

She just sat there, in the door,

And shivered right in front of me.

The little girl, she begged me, "don't."

And then I knew I couldn't leave.

I sat beside her, in the door

And shared a little bit of me.

    Little urchin, in the sea,

    Sea of streets, sea of lights.

    Little urchin, sea of spines,

    Tide comes in, every night.

The little girl, I begged her, "don't."

But when I knew I couldn't leave.

She slipped the knife between my ribs

And took, what once I'd given free.

    Little urchin, in the sea,

    Sea of streets, sea of lights.

    Little urchin, sea of spines,

    Tide comes in, every night.

The little girl, I begged her, "don't,"

Long after I'd begun to leave

For another place. To hear her say

To someone new: "Come sit with me."

    Little urchin, in the sea,

    Sea of streets, sea of lights.

Little urchin, sea of spines,

Tide comes in, every night.

High tide's bringin' me in tonight.

Red tide, but I'll be all right.

(2002)

NINE-AND-A-HALF

The Spear of Longinus is no myth.

With it, I've cast my many javelins

at Heaven.

I've played Achilles, hurling my best

to the stars, and be they near or far,

as a shore on the other side of all the world,

I felled all your gods.

But never won your love.

Whether you went to your knees

for deities below, or above,

no matter how gilded and impotent an idol,

or abusive a tyrant, you gave Thanks

for liberation, then wept

at emptied altars you thought

I could not see.

And all the while me, Achilles,

refusing to play at becoming

your New God.

Be it with the booming voice

of constant command, or simply by

slipping the need of me, like sand

into the spaces, between your toes.

The places you don't fully defend.

And all the while Thought and Memory

of you and me soared the world's skies,

and me, so concerned it's the Memory

of you and me most vulnerable to

being lost.

While I ponder the cost

of choosing to remain Man.

The Spear of Longinus is no myth.

With it, I've pierced my own side.

Hung, half-blind, from the Tree

at the center of the world.

Screaming silent runes,

from a strained throat.

Forever

knowing.

I'll never win

your love.

(2002)

THE EDITOR

"You don't like it?" I offer.

"Well ...," She says.

"You *don't* like it."

We're (desperately) on the lookout for good material, the listing reads. Though why they should advertise at all is beyond me. It is a buyer's market, after all.

She might "solicit." But it's my move that makes whatever I do a "submission."

***

I guess I should be happy She responded personally. No form letter here, with faded, photocopied rationalizations for my judged inadequacy.

But does having a "why" ever really make it better? What good, in the end, when all that it is is an End, is the Reason?

"Feel for me," her gaze implores. Implies that Her job, so much more than mine, is the one that's tough."

Feel for me.

Golden Rule.

(A Golden Shower.)

It doesn't take gold, you know. Just power, of some kind. Over someone else's spirits.

***

And I am enjoined to wonder that, maybe, if I change, you see, work to improve on what She already can't see, She'll give it another shot, another look-see.

But years in the Game have taught me that, if that were true, She already would have said yes. Yes, just maybe with stipulations.

"The wording's too strong," She says. "Look here ... using the word 'soul' ...?"

"How about saying 'heart' ...?" I offer.

"Well, it doesn't matter," she says. "It's still too strong."

***

A bit later, I point out to Her that I thought she liked it that way.

"Yes, but ... "

"'But' what?"

"I guess, now that I've actually seen it, I don't."

How isn't that a lie? I think. But I know arguing this out is no use. Living things change. Perhaps She did want it that way once, but doesn't any more.

Even I change my mind. And how would anyone tell the difference between that and a Lie? I wonder.

***

It doesn't matter, of course. The first rule is to never argue with a Rejection.

***

The next submission, as a matter of course, gets nothing but the form letter.

"This piece just doesn't suit our needs ..." it reads, a photocopy with nothing but a carbon scrawl for a signature, everything sent back in a short three days. As if anticipated, and intercepted upon delivery.

"But thanks for thinking of Us," it makes sure to add.

"No," I write on the blank greeting card, more satisfied. More satisfied than at anything I've created in so long a time, "Thank *You*."

Clear. Succinct. Concrete.

There, you see.

She's made me better already.

GROUND ZERO, AT THE TRINITY TEST SITE

Three Liars made the world.

I wasn't one of Them.

You believe me.

Don't you?

The check's in the mail.

I won't come in your mouth.

I'll only put it in a little.

If it hurts, I'll take it out again.

Of course, though I've pushed the envelope

into a box a time or two,

I've never paid for it

Being delivered, in all my life.

Of course, I have no hope,

of ever again getting

near your lips.

Three Liars made the World.

I wasn't One.

You can't call it a Lie.

You can't catch me,

if I've never had the opportunity

to Fall.

I am

not responsible.

I was never your

Creator, Sustainer, Destroyer,

Father, Son or Ghost.

I wasn't the most deadly thing

you ever let inside you.

Or let slip out.

Three Liars made the world.

I wasn't one of them.

But you stopped believing

in me.

Didn't you?

(2002)

ANGIE'S DEATH

"Get down from that roof," Angie's grandmother called out over the patter of light rain. "Get down from there, before you catch your death."

What grandmother didn't know was that she'd already caught him, Her Death, just the week last. He was in a little gilded birdcage that had lain empty since her parakeet Juan had flown away. Juan had always been a naughty bird, and Angie had to admit she hadn't been sad to see him go.

So now she was sitting and chatting amiably with him, Her Death, in the soft drizzle.

He seemed to like the rain. Angie did too. She always found it romantic.

Still, she couldn't help but shed a little tear for Her Death. Unlike her, he simply looked forlornly into the falling drops, as if lost in bittersweet remembrances.

That was what made Angie remember she had some sugar-cubes, inside. So she scurried in to get her tea service, and her dolls.

Angie was eight now, and knew her doll-friends, such as they were, those of the vacant eyes, could only fill their roles in a tea party if one were to add a touch of imagination. But she hoped Her Death would play along and treat them as real.

There was cause for hope. He couldn't ignore them any more than had Juan.

Yes, naughty, naughty bird. She was glad he was gone.

BIOS (Basic Input Output System) v.7.7

ROBERT SUBIAGA, JR. Case File # 3128221

Fri. 12/13: Patient's Messianic delusions continue. Has created short story with "Goddess" character. Can't determine whether he created her or she created him.

Wed. 12/25: Patient insists I refer to today as 'Wotan's Day' and that he's gouged out one of his eyes to achieve inner vision. I tell him I see no damage. Patient tells me I need to gouge out one of my eyes. I ask him which one. He says, "If you don't know, I can't help you."

Tue. 12/29: Patient has come up with Trinitarian metaphysics, prances tirelessly, singing, "There's Daddy, then Junior, and I'm the Spook!" Off-key rendition spooks other clients indeed.

Fri. 13/1: I ask patient if he knows what sacrilege is. He accuses me of wanting him to say it's a gum resin. I tell him that would be mucilage. "Right," he says. "But you'll find sacrilege holds everything together better."

TRANSPARENT MAN

She sees through me.

Yet is the first of those

who do,

to render me not

Invisible.

(2004)

FLIES THE DUTCHMAN

Sixteen steps from helm to bow,

I pace beneath a flickering sky,

hear a bell across the deck,

hear the toll, to even try.

Seventeen steps, and I'm overboard

Tasting the water, of blood and salts;

a trembling ghost, who learns to swim;

in the sea of unremembered faults.

The Dutchman flies, alone and sails

on waves that wash clean memory.

You're not dead, just more gone;

a living shade to trouble me.

For the bottom I dive, eyes do sting,

Through silt, I grasp, I think your hair

I kick for surface, and the light,

I strain my breath, to share the air.

While the Dutchman flies his woman's jailed,

and wanders free of memory

but you've lost nothing you'll recall;

not even an after-image of me.

Just seaweed tangled in my grip

and even the knots do fall apart,

drift away, as I swim for shore,

swim hard enough to burst my heart.

For the Dutchman's wife, a swimmer wails,

cursed to eternal memory.

capable of losing nothing;

nothing, but a will to be.

For a living ghost a drowned man pales

on the bottom of a bottomless sea.

I won't be me for a long, long time.

But in the end, me it will be.

(2004)

OF FLESH, & THE SPIRIT

"What would you do if I left you?" She says.

"You can never leave me," I say.

There is the returning momentary flash of rage in Her eyes. The one that asks how dare I. Accuse me of being controlling.

But She avoids confrontation now and just changes the subject. "When will I finally meet your parents?" She says.

I shrug.

"Who are they, anyway?"

I say nothing. I don't know.

Sometimes, to suit her, to suit me, I've made up stories. I'm not proud of it. But I've made up stories.

And I really don't know.

Just as She never knew Hers.

"I'd better meet them," She laughs sardonically. "Someday." Then: "After all, we have to make sure they're not mine, too."

I shrug again. Who knows? They could be.

Twins, separated at birth. If it weren't for the fact that we can't be separated.

Even though controlling is hardly the word. Not when in no way are either of us active in pulling the other back.

Just attached at the hip. So to speak

Dead weight.

***

On Day Two, She whispers in shock.

As I said, I've often made up stories. And I'm rather good at it. It's one thing, at least, one can say I contribute to the relationship.

Solidity, yet complexity. Sensual detail. A relief from the boredom of predictability, and ostensible perfection.

Often enough, She'll skirt closer into the hollow of my shoulder and chest and lounge there, lost in the smell or an orange, or the palette of a sunset.

Until She wants more. More than stories, at which time She'll run. More stories, if She is not to.

"It's a *long* story," I warn her.

"And I have all the Time in the world," She says.

I look at Her questioningly.

"I do," She says. "Maybe you don't, but I do."

Then She whispers, uncertainly, and most of all trying to hide the uncertainty. "I'm sure I do."

***

And it was the evening and the morning. Third Day. Hump day.

"Do you really expect me to believe that?" She says when I finish my latest tale. "You're so funny sometimes."

"Funny funny or funny strange?" I ask.

She gives it some serious thought and says, "Both."

***

Four Days now. And She tells me to stop brooding.

She isn't planning of abandoning me. She isn't planning on leaving.

Well, not yet. Maybe someday. But not now. And if I'm insecure about that, too bad, perhaps someday will come sooner.

But She says, with something like an attempt as reassurance: "I keep you around, don't I?"

"I'm always around," I both correct Her and agree with Her. Anything but insecure in that. Alas.

But She's convinced otherwise, so for the latest of countless times, I humor Her. Play the Game.

Ask, "Why?"

"Why what?"

"Why do you, you know ... 'keep me around.'"

She doesn't answer. I don't think She knows.

***

Fifth Day.

She's nudged me in my rib. Or perhaps between them.

This one hurt. Like a spear.

"That's not me," She says.

"It's always you," I say. "There's no one else but us here."

"I think I know when I do something," She says petulantly. And uncertainly.

She rarely knows Her own strength.

Even if usually it means She overestimates it.

***

The Sixth Day, like clockwork, She starts out with a "I don't know why I ever get the urge to wander." Feeling out the waters again.

It's in Your nature, I almost tell Her. Just as much as it is never to succeed.

***

"Still …"

"Still what?" I say.

"What *would* you do if I left you?"

"You can never leave me," I say.

But silly me. Seventh Day, and hoping She'd give it a rest.

When all it can do is just start, all over again.

WOLVES TALES, 4

Black wolf, lone wolf,

pad the snows, glide, through,

stiff tree limbs that slide

off, and embrace not

the ghost, who knows.

Pad the snows, leave little

trace, but eyes that stare, quiet,

long; grace nothing, 'til

it's the not-nothing that negates,

until it treads into

the something where there can be:

no empty spaces.

Cougar-hiss, near-miss, eagle-chase;

but in wolf-territory, the long face

says: I but let you chase.

At cougar, birds laugh. But wait,

the cat-hiss and bird-chuckle grates:

For it is not I, they both say,

that to hunt big game, requires mates.

Am I ghost then, now? black wolf

ponders his fate, or is there one,

somewhere, but of late

unremembering?

Lone wolf, black wolf, September

breeze cloak or January snow tracks,

see the one that should be mate, chained

to that shack, in her master's lawn.

How? you ask, irate, *is it*

that one should make boundaries,

in wolf-territories?

Until the moon rises, you wait.

But she howls not to you,

no matter how late.

She whines for *his* touch, eyes dull,

no shine, unremembering a time, when

... Is this her fate?

A boundary, and you,

wolf, without dowry, to placate

this "master" of hers. *What disaster*

has befallen you? you pant, *that I should*

pay for you, or you seek permission,

for my memories of our laughter?

Her two-legged "man," never to be

aught but a boy; not even tamed dog

but sheep, in wolf's clothing.

Yet who has conditioned, and toyed,

with her from as a pup, for years, 'til

she fears, only his every rejection.

Comes for him only. Makes herself

come for his beckoning.

And beyond barbed-wire wall,

you, wolf, asks: have you really

forgotten who you are? Or did he

ever let you know at all?

But she barks, and even you,

Wolf, hates, blindly; and, panting after,

licks the dirt of this "man," this "master."

Her eyes wan, and sticks to his side

ever after.

Stale now her every sense of smell,

and tastes, but for this actor.

So much lost, but the cost borne by

the ghost you are, padding snows,

your own master, beyond boundaries.

Taking issue, with all boundaries.

When it is all

wolf-territory.

Good dog, the boy scratches

her ear, tells her, to assuage

her fear: *Good dog.*

Not so, you, wolf, knows.

But she knows not, And so it goes.

(2004)

MEPHISTO, AT THE BELLAGIO

Sin.

I wish sin *was* in. Really.

Like in my blood, you know.

But I'm just one of those silly libertines,

who dreams of loosing dragons

from depths I claim are mine.

When it's all just

fairy tales, and fortified wine.

When the steps needed, the divine choosing

of a throbbing pulse over a cool glance,

that's something I haven't chanced

to really learn.

Let alone master.

I fake it well.

Maybe that's why I haven't come to

hate this town yet.

This place where a whore, and more, some stupid,

backbreaking bet are portrayed as the inevitable

result of every sunset denouement.

Yet …

Not for the Dealer.

And maybe, too, after all the years

I've come to learn that's the healing

role for me.

That I belong out of the Game,

except as prophet of the House.

Let the Great Wheel spin,

but I'm getting off.

I'll but turn the cards, bodhisattva

of a New Tarot.

"You know, there's no telling

how far you can go if you let someone else

take the credit." There, I said it.

Even though the credit for that quote belongs

to a broken clock that would be

lucky to be right even twice a day.

But I am out of the Game, girls.

I swear. (I Am.)

I'll but spin the Wheel,

but I'm getting off.

Maybe after I help you

get off, too.

And when I take my rake—

when my swift hand snakes out

to slip your lost chips my way—

don't hate me for it.

I lost my soul. Eons before

you could even know the distinction

between the Dark and the Day.

Lost what was never mine,

never even … really there. Playin'

with the House's roll.

And so I don't *really* want to steal

all you own. Maybe just a little.

For Old Time's sake.

(2004)

MOURNING LIGHT

I am at the Carnival, but in my mind I see
the old farm-house. We're in the city now,
in a park, but we used to have carnivals just
like this pass through the nearest small town
when I was a girl, and the contrasts blending
to similarity don't seem odd. They seem
natural.

Our house was on the edge of a marsh. The
evening I recall it I was crouching among
the reeds, in the snow as I remember not
being wet, and I looked up at a lone light in
the kitchen, just as that light blinked off.
Then I slunk through the grass and reeds,
low to the ground.

I narrate in my head. *I remember my childhood,
more vividly than the past few years, when so
much has changed.*

I remember my dogs, Spritzer and Brandy. Spritzer
was really old by the time I started junior high, and
she was blind and arthritic and in so much pain.
Then, one night, she just went off into the swamp

to die alone. We looked and looked, but couldn't find her.

I cried so very hard that, when Brandy got really old and sick couple years later, Daddy said he was going to take her to the hospital. She wagged her tail and tried in vain to still play ball, just before he took her away.

He never knew I understood that he wasn't shooting at a crow the next morning, when I heard his gun.

I lie down in the swamp, waiting for the frost to whiten the grass around me.

Lies. The world is built on lies.

***

Dusk settles over the small, travelling carnival, and blinking hues of scarlets, emeralds and golds from the artificial lights start to provide more appropriate accompaniment to the carnies and hucksters. And laughing spectators.

I go around the trailers at the fringe of the carnival, giving none of my attention to the merriment or the music fading into the background. I'm focused on the stuffed bear in hand. I squeeze him reassuringly as I peer around a corner.

"Hey, little boy. Are you lost?"

At least that's how I picture it. But it's not me.

I'm somewhere else, in front of a game booth, two women wait near a hawker. He keeps harassing them. "Just play one more game." Win a teddy bear. Lisa ignores him. Haughty faux-Eurotrashy hipster bitch. Why wouldn't she? It only turns him on to the chase more. I, on the other hand, look around nervously.

"Where can he *be?*" I ask for the sixth time in as many minutes.

"Come on, Krissy love," Lisa coos. "It shouldn't be that much a concern of your pretty little head. He's my man, after all."

I shake my head, sardonically amused as always even if as always she makes me despise her. The same trick she pulls on men who can't resist her. I turn away and continue to scan the surroundings to break the spell.

At the fringes of the carnival, a dark-haired, light-skinned man in a trench coat stands near a trailer. He pulls out a pack of cigarettes and a lighter. Suddenly his eyes narrow, though no other part of him reacts, though he has to know that something is coming up on him fast. But instead, calmly, Thorpe turns in that direction. And whatever might have been coming, if it were there, knows better and veers away.

In front of the hawker's booth, I say "You can have him, 'love.' But I doubt he really belongs to anyone."

***

"Are you lost?" Somewhere I see myself under a carnival trailer. Just my legs visible in the dim light, and a little blood. Julian, dear boy, walks past on the other side of trailer. Walks past and picks up a teddy bear.

In front of the game booth but looking outward my whole body goes slack as I see, in the distance, a scrawny, skittish mutt of a camp dog. Little more than a pup. Slowly, trying to be careful not to scare the thing, I approach with an outstretched hand.

"Here, boy. Come on. Are you lost?"

It shivers, ready to bolt.

"Can I help you find your home?"

It growls, unconvincingly. So unconvincing even to itself that it quickly becomes a whimper.

Wherever Thorpe stands lighting a cigarette, sweet little Julian approaches with his new teddy. The boy walks up and stands next to Thorpe, exaggerated mannerisms showing how he tries to emulate Thorpe's plays at "cool" and "tough." Thorpe looks down, wry, deadpan, Julian's attempts only a bit validated. Sweet kid never understands underneath it all he's as much despised for trying to be like Thorpe as anything.

Shrugging and smiling, the boy offers Thorpe the teddy bear the way someone would offer a hunter a trophy.

I approach Lisa with my scared pup cowering, but not fighting me, in my arms. Lisa looks around for a glimpse of Thorpe and shrugs, disinterested. Thorpe, for his part, appears with the boy at his side. In one smooth motion he tosses the teddy bear to Lisa, walking by us both without looking and without breaking stride. Julian following in lockstep like a toy soldier.

Lisa gives the teddy bear a glance but I'm the one who notices a small smear of blood on the teddy bear's back.

"Good God, Thorpe—what the hell is this from?"

He shrugs. "Bad neighborhood, dear."

"I mean it, Thorpe!"

Thorpe puffs in a casual manner on his cigarette. Then he smiles wider, his teeth intentionally showing. He leans against a trailer and starts to whittle a long stick to a sharp point.

"Ask the boy."

I lean down to Julian and look him in the face, stroking the dog. It's not irredeemably afraid of Julian either; unlike I'm sure its reaction to Lisa and Thorpe. Between that and my own gaze Julian melts a little, as I figured he would.

"Julian…," I say softly. "What is this from?"

Julian pauses, his gaze shifting from Thorpe to me and the pup, then back again. God, Thorpe fucks with this kid so. So much that Julian still acts the kid, when he should've outgrown that a while ago. So torn.

He tries to look away from me and shrugs. Doesn't realize that not only isn't it cool when Thorpe does it but the kid can't even make it look cool.

I ask him again. "Sweetheart, what is this blood from?"

"I dunno," he says. "Maybe a dead animal. I guess."

Thorpe drops the whittling stick—end nice and sharp—and Julian pauses for a moment before bounding away to his side. Julian picks up the stake and continues the whittling job.

Together they walk out of the carnival, through the fog that's rolling in.

Lisa shoots me a triumphant glance before joining them.

I see myself lying under a carnival trailer. I know I should go look for myself. But I see a quivering dog in my arms and know I'll have to let him go if I go do, and I'll probably never convince him to come back. So I pick up the blood-marked teddy bear too and just go join the people I came with in leaving.

***

Rogue is as avant-garde as always. I never knew why this was the kind of restaurant Jordan fell in love with. Or at least fell in love with bringing me to. Here he sits, blonde and tousled and making me think "All American" even in a country fast browning, looking like he should be wearing a letter jacket even though he looks like he should be in grad school, and we are at an overly formally set table with baroque fusion dishes all over the menu and a loud gesticulating and oh-so-hip poet in a far corner trying to win the latest slam.

Lisa walks in and joins a man at a table for two. She smiles at him and they kiss. I can't tell if she's here to watch us or playing predator is just an accidental perk of her pre-existing date. Bitch.

"I hope you don't mind, but I ordered for you, too.

Order for her. A woman doesn't like to be forced but she likes a man who takes charge. Probably dating advice from Kris and Thorpe, which she can watch and see how it works.

I play along. "Jordan, you know I don't the same appetite as you for—"

Jordan smiles knowingly at her and tips his head. OK, so Mr. Clean Cut might not have ordered something experimental. I respond in kind, suppressing a quizzical smile.

"What *did* you order?" I ask.

Jordan nods at the approaching waiter, who places a full dinner plate in front of him but only a Bloody Mary before me.

"Smart-ass," I laugh.

"Guilty."

I nod at his lavish plate. "Just save that appetite then," I tell him. "If you want tonight to be special."

***

If you want tonight to be special. I come to regret saying that.

We made small talk. But Jordan's answers grew ever more perfunctory and noncommittal, and I could tell he was wondering if, when it came to what he meant of as special, I was just teasing him again. No, not teasing. Tormenting. Eventually he stared at me without even realizing it, not aggressive but with puppy eyes, trying to bring up a heavier topic that has been avoided too long, but just gets heavier and more avoided because of it.

I never hold his serious gaze long enough to give him a chance.

Finally, Jordan looks down shyly and speaks softly. "So? What do you think?"

I've become irritated. Again. "You know what my answer is. I'm not ready"

"C'mon," he says, trying to be sarcastic. Trying to be a little commanding. "It could be fun."

This time I don't want my man presuming to order for me. "A barrel of laughs," I fairly snarl. "A regular riot."

He curls up as though I've smacked his nose with a newspaper. "Forget that I joked about it," he says, now pleading. "I *need* this from you, Kris." Then he shows just how "All-American" he really still is. "If you really loved me—"

"*If I really loved you*—?" My jaw clenches. "You bastard." My nostrils flare. I like the feeling. I hate the situation, but if I'm going to be in this situation I love the feeling. Letting the animal out. "Damn you, Jordan," I say under my breath. "*Love* isn't one explosive moment. Love is *eternal*."

"Don't you see? That's what I'm talking about."

My eyes water. No. I don't see.

"I told you how I feel about all this," I say. "I told you too. No matter how hard it is to believe, for someone as old as me, but this … this is my first time."

This seems to make an impression on him, and he becomes evasive. Trying to change the subject. Why is that so unsatisfying, I wonder, even infuriating, when just dropping it is what I've been working for these past few moments?

We eat in silence for about thirty seconds. Then he starts fidgeting. "I called you last night," he says, trying to sound nonchalant. "But you didn't answer. What'd you do?"

I glance over to Lisa's table, but she's nowhere to be seen.

Back at the apartment, we smoked. Jordan just a little weed. Me far too many cigarettes. My mother's voice in my head from the first time she caught me lighting up a used butt. What, do you think no matter what you'll live forever?

My place, as usual, is in disarray. Clothing litters a trail on the floor to the bed. But we just sit on the bed, staring at each other.

"I . . . I'm sorry," I say. Sorry I couldn't go through with it. "I thought I could tonight. But—"

"Forget it," he says. Broken. "There's always tomorrow." Always tomorrow is what I always tell him, but he says it without conviction.

I punch and slap him playfully. Tickle him until he starts to laugh.

"There," I say. "That's *better*." I smile mischievously. "After all, we don't have to wait 'til tomorrow for everything."

Embrace. Kiss passionately. Falling to the bed and start to undress each other. Be creative.

Bring him to orgasm, without the stress of thinking there's a certain way things have to be.

But afterward, the wetness on him staying warm instead of growing cold, simply because it's trapped between our bodies as he spoons me from behind. Desperately clutching and infantile even in his sleep. Crying without even knowing it, and probably not even knowing why.

***

When I finally fade off things stay lucid. I know Thorpe and Lisa are watching outside the window of my apartment. They were there long before the lights went out.

"Think she'll finally do it?" Lisa asks.

Bitterly, Thorpe says, "She'd *better*."

***

About 2 A.M. I wake. Light a few candles. Play faint music. Jordan wakes, momentarily looking vibrant, and we kiss as though we're about to devour each other. I think things have changed and just bask in our nakedness and the glow, but when we pull our faces away I see the clouds coming back into Jordan's face.

This, all we have, is not enough again.

And again I've had enough of him making me feel guilty about it and break our embrace, get up, and walk toward the window. Hug myself, angry that he won't hug me, not and just appreciate it for what it is, and shiver.

"Jordan—I've got to think. Maybe I can't go through with this at all. Not with you."

"You're still frightened," says. But I feel his shock. I've gone from having cold feet and telling him to wait, to outright denying him ever. Now a girl with cold feet is infinitely more preferable and he's trying to pull me back to where he was in torment by being understanding. Only because he has to.

"I'm going out for a while," I say, dressing. "I'll be back."

"Kris—wait!" he says. "You're not leaving me, are you? It is *me* you want to be with, isn't it?"

God. What irony. "Shouldn't that be what I'm asking you?" I put to him.

I throw her coat on and walks past the bed to leave, but Jordan, kneeling on the bed, lunges outward to throw his arms around my waist, with tears in his eyes.

"And if I refused to let you go?"

More cold than I've ever been, I tell him, "I'd break your arms."

***

Julian sits in an abandoned alleyway, tucked in a dark doorway. In his hands is the stake that Thorpe had been whittling at the carnival. On the opposite end of the crude, brutal point, Julian is carving intricate and beautiful designs into the "handle."

360

Suddenly a wind whips down the alley and blows loose debris in front of it. Julian looks up in interest and hides deeper in the doorway's shadows.

***

That's when I come upon him, walking the street as if looking for something. But I don't know what. I know I must appear as distraught as I am; disheveled and hugging myself as though I'm cold even as sweat is on my forehead and upper lip.

Then I see the dog—the very same one from the carnival—standing in the middle of the alley. Perhaps it followed Julian after we left. But it isn't over with him.

It whines at me. I hesitate and the dog continues to whine. But as I take my first step toward the animal, it lunges away and runs.

Crushed by this I walk away, not even thinking to say hi to Julian, wondering what he must think of me as he watches me go.

***

I'm betting it was about 4:30 AM, me having been back to see Jordan sleeping and then gone again, when he must have awakened in an empty bed to see those glowing red numbers of the clock guide him to my note by our bedside. What did he think as he read it? My apologies and signature telling him to meet me at the Rogue Restaurant at about 9:00 P.M.?

The only thing not crossing his mind being that it might not have been from me at all.

***

Another poetry reading is going on when he gets there, but this time the crowd's reaction to the crass humor of the present reader is hostile. The waiter lights another candle at the table where Jordan waits.

Suddenly Thorpe approaches and sits.

Jordan turns away. Love advice from Thorpe's slick partner Lisa is something Jordan has never been loath to listen to, but for some odd reason he's always hated her partner in crime.

"Jordan?" Thorpe says.

No reaction.

"Jordan, ignoring me won't make me go away."

"This is between me and Kris," Jordan fumes. "You stay out of it."

Thorpe pulls a quarter from his pocket. With uncanny dexterity, he twirls it in and over his fingers like a magician preparing a trick. Then, in the middle of this, he snaps his hands closed, the quarter apparently in one of the two fists he holds out.

"Pick a hand," he says.

Jordan glares at Thorpe, tired of the childish games. Even though I'd warned him many a time that when it came to Thorpe there was nothing childish about him, simply predatory.

"Just pick a hand."

Jordan picks one hand. It's empty.

But now he picks the other and it's empty too.

"Guess you've been playing the wrong game, eh?" Thorpe says. "What good's the 'right' strategy then?"

Jordan looks away, trying to ignore Thorpe again. But the hook is set.

Under his breath, but sly and sweet, Thorpe starts reeling. "Oh, just the brave little soldier now, aren't we? Come on—do you still want a taste from infinity's well . . . just once more?" Thorpe chuckles. "Bah. Amateur. What could you have ever done with immortality anyway?"

Jordan turns and fixes a cold and unyielding gaze directly on Thorpe.

"Look who's talking," he says. Jordan's backbone shows itself. "When you've never gone where I'm going either."

Thorpe looks away now, chagrined. Then he recovers and speaks slyly again.

"Come now, friend. I'm a hell of a lot older than you."

"Doesn't mean jack until you've been where I am," Jordan challenges him.

"I've seen this done countless times—*done* this for others countless times," Thorpe says. "Hell," he sneers, "I'd even do it for you, if I thought you were my type.

"Your point?"

"No, you hick little putz, I haven't been where you are. But I have been where Kris is. If you want to convince her … I'm the one to ask how."

Realization dawns on Jordan. Not the particulars of what Thorpe and Lisa have done to me, but the gist.

"Where's Kris?" Jordan demands, but knowing all the power is in the other court.

Thorpe smiles knowingly.

"*Waiting*," he says.

***

The dark cellar is composed of old, rough-hewn bricks with trickles of water dripping along them. A couple torches cast flickering light. Lisa approaches me, where I'm chained to a wall with heavy iron fetters. Lisa toys with the stake that Thorpe had whittled then Julian had been carving. She paints intricate patterns on the ornate handle.

Then Lisa takes a chalice-like cup and drinks deep, blood spilling out from the corners of her mouth. She then holds the cup out to me, but intentionally just outside her reach.

"Getting hungry, darling? I think this one was a Frenchman—Brittany, maybe 1956. A *very* good year."

I look away, disgusted.

"You cannot deny who you are, Kristina," she says to me. "*What* you are." Then she turns serious. "Or deny the responsibilities to yourself, to the rest of us, the being in the Family entails."

"Jordan's life is no joke to me," I say. Tasting my own blood through cracked lips. Wondering how long I can last without something to drink.

Lisa tempts me with the chalice again. "Don't worry, love. Dinner's on its way. Just do what's necessary."

Lisa drops the strange wooden stake within reach of me, letting me pick it up. My grip trembles. Lisa turns her back on me.

"Or not," she says coyly. "The options are all yours."

***

The entryway winds through an old warehouse. Thorpe leads Jordan through. Shadowy figures step out from behind beams and pillars to eye him before retreating back, forming a "gauntlet" he must move through. The figures are all slightly freakish—too pale, or dressed in long-gone fashions. Faintly, the carnival music plays.

Julian chases Jordan and Thorpe at a distance, as if trying to catch glimpses of something taboo, and yet too terrifying for him to want to see.

As Jordan and Thorpe pass through an open area on the warehouse floor, a group of wailing figures in black robes surround him, keening like mourners at an ancient Celtic funeral or like the women on the road in Christ's Passion. Jordan stops for a moment, catching glimpses of a few figures deeper in the warehouse.

One is the young woman, the one I never saw killed, but who Julian took at the carnival. She sits on a windowsill, staring out, though nothing is visible through the window's frosted glass, probably still in shock at the small boy who seduced her. For some brought in that way it takes a while to get over the guilt of being pleasured against one's will by being killed. Worse when it happens at the hands of one who appears a child— and whose frozen motives sometimes are in line with that even while fully adult motives mix in over the years. As much as I love Julian I'm angered at him as he creeps up to the still dazed and confused co-ed. Cradling his head between her breasts treads to border of violation, but when he pulls her top down and suckles fresh blood from bites around her nipples, wracking her with climaxes even while she's too confused to fend him off, sensations that will only prolong her confusion for months or even years, part of me wants to give him the mother figure he longs for with a spanking.

But I'm not the only mentor he's had. Thorpe comes over and, if only for a minute or so, adds to the young blonde's torment by attending to her other breast. Thankfully, it's only a dalliance, and he soon stops to pat Julian on the head and call him a good boy before going back to playing ringmaster for the main event. And a feeling of forgiveness comes over me as Julian leaves his poor co-ed alone as he eyes Jordan coming through, the boy starting to weep.

Sadly the woman at the windowsill is too new to feel part of the Family. Now near-catatonic, she slices her own wrist nonchalantly starts to suckle on it. It provides her with no less pleasure than before, but at least on her terms, and she curls into a fetal ball on the windowsill and moans as she pleasures herself.

A second group of the figures converges on Jordan. These keep some distance and stand or pace with folded arms and cold glances, paying him only slight attention, like ancient warriors demanding courage of one chosen for sacrifice.

This group gives way to another, who dance around Jordan, drinking greedily from chalices, blood flowing down the sides of their mouths. They proffer their chalices to him, just out of reach and continue a combination of wailing and laughing that seems like a rowdy crowd at an Irish wake. Jordan comes down an elevator shaft, and the crowd parts like a veritable Red Sea to let him and his escort pass.

But as soon as Jordan steps out of the elevator, he turns to find the crowd, inexplicably, gone.

"We come into the world alone," he whispers with a faint smile. "And it's how we leave."

And then he walks in on me.

***

The room is completely white now. Fresh paint splattered on all the walls. I'm still chained, but with a long line of slack loosed.

One moment we hear cacophonies outside.
Music. Drumming. Chanting. Heartbeats as
loud as any. Passion, love, lust, and death in
the air. The next instant all is silent. Not as if
the drummers and musicians and singers
have stopped. There still would be panting,
breathing, a scrape of a foot. The pure
silence that they are not there and never
were.

Jordan walks slowly toward me. I shake,
sweaty and hollow-eyed, wanting to protest.
Tell him to go away. I'm not ready. It's my
first time. I've never done this to someone
before.

"This isn't exactly what I expected," he says, his
soft voice trying to soothe me. No longer
desperate. Composed and hard even in the
softness. I've never wanted him more. "But maybe
these things never are what you expect," he says.

"I don't … don't want … to do this … !" I say.

"Yes," he says. "Yes, you do. For me you do."

Jordan walks within range. He kneels like a
willing sacrifice and turns his head to bare
his neck. His pulse throbs and it's nectar to
me.

I want him. I want him so badly. I want to
own that pulse.

***

Jordan looks up at me again from his knees, then bows his head and gives a pained smile. The kind that make his own fangs clearly visible instead of how he so often deftly hides then.

I looks up helplessly, tears streaming down my face as I drive the stake home.

Where the heart is.

***

Julian watches from a high window of the warehouse as I exit into the alley. I walk to the car where Thorpe and Lisa wait.

Limousine with blackened windows. As if this were a party.

I open the limo door and pause there.

"It's rough, dear," Lisa says, "But we had to do it this way. We didn't think you were going to go through with it."

"Speak for yourself," Thorpe says from the far side of the rear seat, showing his arousal by his hand snaking up under Lisa's skirt. "Some like it rough."

Lisa tries to take the edge off with sympathy in her voice as she tells him, "speak for yourself, you bastard." But not too much. She doesn't move Thorpe's hand and half-closes her eyes as she rotates slightly against it.

I want to feel sick. But there's a pain beyond which nausea won't intrude. I look about at the city slowly and vacantly, obviously uninterested in their half-assed attempts to allay grief.

"We knew you had it in you," Thorpe says.

I stare icily at him. "Oh? I think you didn't have a clue."

"You *don't* understand," Lisa says. "But you will, someday."

I've heard it before. Heard of what none of us have the strength to do ourselves. And it all makes sense, twisted sense, even to me now. How hard it is to give up something we've had so much of. When there has been so much to see. So many pleasures to be had.

There is too much of a history of hope. Even when we're too tired to hope any more.

We all need release. We all just need someone else to do the releasing.

When the ghost of immortality won't let go unless it can be someone we can love.

I watch Thorpe unable to have the decency to wait a while before fingering Lisa in the back of the limo, and her acting as if pretending I can't see means I can't and think those two might live forever. Well, or at least until they meet with an accident.

Too bad that's not enough to give me purpose. I smile at that thought, and then smile again that Thorpe and Lisa no doubt think their words have had a positive impact on me.

Something happens to give me a real smile though. The alley had been empty but the scrawny dog from the carnival appears yet again. It pads down the alley slowly, at a pace where, this time, I might easily catch up.

I shut the limo door softly and begin to walk toward him.

Amazed, Thorpe and Lisa roll down the tinted window scream at me.

"Where are you going?!"

"For God's sake, Kris, it's almost dawn!"

I stop long enough to half-turn back and muse: "Good. I think I'd like to see the sunrise."

There is a lightness in my step I haven't had for a long time as I start up again, then call back, "Feel free to join me."

Thorpe and Lisa scramble to get the window back up as the first faint rays of sunlight wash over the horizon. While Julian watches me from the window of the warehouse.

I can't say I could hide the beginnings of pain from my face as the first rays hit me, even from a distance. In fact, I know I stumbled once or twice.

But that part is hard to remember compared to the joy when I heard Julian burst from the door of the warehouse and run to my side.

He took my hand. I couldn't see him exactly, as I turned to him, with the light already burning away my eyes. But I felt him there, until I could feel no more. Everything fading to white.

The last sensation hearing the dog barking happily behind us, not quite comprehending, just asking where we were going.

Don't worry boy. Where you're going too. Eventually.

But take your time.

STONES

"Stones would play/ inside her head.

And where she slept/ they made her bed...."

When I was a child, no matter how well I did in Sunday School, I could never escape the twists and turns of realizing:

I'm growing up with a doctrine about incarnation that makes me wonder how God isn't Reality's most cosmic ... motherfucker.

And the scarcely suppressed urge to joke that "God" isn't what dyslexic philosophers try to get not to defecate on the carpet.

That soft, white plush their blue-collar parents always dreamt they'd have when they sent the kid to the best Ivy League schools, thinking he'd wind up a doctor or lawyer. An engineer, maybe. At least a securities broker.

Something … respectable.

Gods usually shit on the carpet anyway.

No more cognizant of the aspirations of parents than of their children; only knowing their masters have left them alone for too long, a poor dumb God, with no better way to deal with His anxiety than to whine, plaintively. To tear apart toilet paper, and paper towels, and newspaper.

Especially newspaper. Everything He can get His hands on, until everything is in tatters, not a Word is left unfragmented, or unsmudged.

I wish I knew what it is with Gods and paper.

I don't own Gods that often. Though there was that once, in college.

My three roommates outvoted me on whether to get one. You can guess who wound up taking care of Him though.

Letting Him out when He needed to void His bladder, His bowels. Playing with Him when He was ready to come back in.

He was a smart God, though, and I could roughhouse with Him, wrestle and grapple, try out my judo, my arms protected against His bite by a heavy leather jacket as I sought to trip Him up. But for all the ferocity of our struggle, all I had to do was give Him the signal that it was all over, that it was time for Him to calm down, sit quietly. And He would.

Discipline your Gods well. They'll only love you the more for it.

He was a mixed breed. Shepherd, mostly. Same kind of mix, if a remarkably different in appearance, as a God I had in grade school. Big brute of a thing, that one.

My grandmother understood what that earlier God meant to me. *Baba*, we called her. My grandmother, I mean. The name means "Old Woman" in the language of her homeland, and I guess it was just a dialectical thing, but others whose ethnicity is from that part of the world often look shocked when I tell about her.

To them it means something like "old fish wife," and is a pejorative. They call their grandmother's a diminutive like *babushka*, or *babunya*, or *babucya*. Which in turn I find funny, since those kids around in in that community of immigrants and children and grandchildren of refugees—especially the upper-class—who used those diminutives often had grandmothers who were blowhards, or stern, or at the very least, even if passive in their aggression, judgmental. And mine was none of these.

Not that I should have known properly. We not only were of poor stock, after all, "uneducated," but on top of it all I was, well, a half-breed. Not even—horror upon horrors—fully "white."

It's probably why I grew up calling the small, earthy but kindly old woman who nurtured me by the title many reserved for a fearsome famous witch.
(Even as I never pointed out to them the curiosity I found, in my uneducated education, that so many other cultures use the same word for "Father." Go figure.)

My grandfather, Baba's husband, *Dyid*, had endured many of the same things, having gone on the run with Baba in the early years, from just before the War on through it. Communists, fascists, my grandparents wanted nothing with either Side. Especially not, as *Dyid* once put it, made to take a gun and go kill someone who had never done him harm.

Burly, he was, with a thick powerful form that I eventually inherited, to blend incongruously with my own father's Pacific genetics; yet *Dyid* was a steadfast pacifist of his own. From the heart too, not any educated streak of ideological passion.

It was in the last camp, where my mother was born, they ultimately ended up. Only many years later, piecing together images from the stories told in Ukrainian—with great reticence in telling anything—was I detective enough to realize it was Flossenbürg concentration camp and/or its satellites.

But it was there that my grandfather saw the theologian Dietrich Bonhoeffer hanged. And that was where *Dyid*'s story of executed "German partisans" in the last days of the War was from.

Yet though Baba and *Dyid* had been in the same camps, ultimately those guarded by Gods—all those not pinschers definitely shepherds—he, but somehow not his wife, had developed a deathly fear of large Gods.

Dyid would come by and see in and try to feed that huge loveable lug of a young God I had, interact with him, but memories of similar Gods meant to subjugate with force and threat kept my own gentle giant of a grandfather on edge.

Even when the brute God wanted to play and be affectionate, *Dyid*'s underlying terror would cause subtle rejection. Which I'm sure that that God picked up on it, and responded in kind, until a vicious feed-forward cycle ruined everything.

But that first God of mine, so powerful and knowing no better, was still one that, somehow, Baba still had no fear of.

Maybe she was a Great Witch, after all. One everybody laughed at, and disparaged as low-born and impotent—when they thought they could. Yet underneath it all … whose very name they feared. But whom I could never laugh at, and would never fear.

Anyway, Baba would bring over good eats for that first God of mine; none of the prepackaged, usual God-food for Him. Huge roasting pans of leftovers from her own table: a lot of rice, and potatoes, and gravy—but always meat.

Baba was, as I said, empathic to the point of easily breaking down in tears of compassion for anyone else's pain. Even if a slightly stocky woman—at least by her later years, after a lifetime's manual labors—of deceptive strength and especially endurance. The kind who not only would never want to hurt a soul, but for any soul to hurt any other. A *bodhisattva*, who would never learn the word. Of actual Infinite Compassion.

But still, meat. Baba knew. Gods are natural carnivores.

She didn't judge me. But neither did she judge Him, or demand He be anything other than what He was.

I loved being at her house. In her kitchen, with her cooking. She fed me well too. Better than anyone before, or since. It was my refuge.

And He was the light of my life, this quirky brute of a God, one of the only such lights after Father moved out.

That is, until my mother's lover got rid of Him.

Story is my God barked during the day, and our neighbor worked nights, and started making threats and calling the police. I don't know if that was all so true. The neighbor never complained where I saw or heard. And Mother's new man—who may have become her husband of many later years but to whom I would never for too many good reasons call "father"—wasn't the kind to care all that much about his neighbor, anyway.

Perhaps he felt my God barked too much at him.

In any event, that God was mine, and that was enough for Him to be hated by this faux-Father. I came home one day, from school, and my God was gone.

That God I had in college was gone soon too. I could see it would happen, which is why I voted against getting one in the first place.

College being such a fluid time, we roommates were sure to part ways soon enough. Hell, the God Himself was given the name of "Stones," and not simply for his coloring, but the recreational profile of those roommates.

Stones would play/ inside her head

And where she slept/ they made her bed ...

(The funniest karma associated with that being the time those roommates pooled their resources for a whole ounce of cannabis and left it on the coffee table—an ill-named piece of furniture in this case if ever there were one—while going out a few minutes and leaving behind a nervous Stones. Who ate all the pot.)

But, as each of us roommates eventually found new places to live, it was more likely than not that it was somewhere Gods weren't allowed. Sure enough, we had to give ours away. I'm the one who didn't want to get one in the first place, and I think I was the only one who was all that bothered when He had to go.

I heard He went to some farm out in the country, where Gods are allowed to run free.

Stones almost got Himself put to death, though, when on the first day one of the first things He did was kill fifteen fowl. Ducks, or maybe it was chickens.

But He redeemed Himself with the irate farmer by the third day. The neighboring farm had a pair of Dobermans that had been terrorizing the children of the farmer who had adopted Stones, especially at the school bus stop. Fearlessly, our God chased those two big, vicious Gods from the farm next door all the way home and protected the children.

That was so many years ago now. Decades. For the life of a God that means it's just about certain He's dead by now.

Sometimes I wonder how.

I wonder if He had someone there, for Him. Someone to scratch behind His ears gently, holding him, while that needle slipped into the vein, just under the skin.

Kind of like Baba died, in my arms, on a spring night not too far from Easter. Strange spring snow falling outside windows that would not open. No matter how many doors had closed.

And She would ache/ for love

and get/ but Stones ...

A good God deserves that much.

You can keep all your bullshit about how to treat a God. Keep all the stores that specialize in high-priced, jewel-studded God-collars for Him.

Keep your high-tech electronic tracking chips so you can find your God when He gets lost.

To hell with millions of brands of kibble for Him, agonizing over them as if it makes a difference— just because all the other God-owners do.

Me? I'll wonder whose really there for Him at the End.

Who will sit there with Him when there is no one else. Stroke His time-wearied head softly. Give Him an embrace.

Grace Him with one last kiss.

When Time comes, as it must, to ease, and speed, a poor bastard's passage, out of this world.

ANTON LEVAY, SEEN AT THE COFFEE BEAN & TEA LEAF, IN HIS DOTAGE

The Satanist wore a cowboy's flowered shirt
And a choker, and had a Sioux quirt, with which
he drove seven midnight stallions through
the hidden dimensions stacked like glass panes,
in the coffee shop.

Where we were surrounded by windows, without
shades, without frames, incapable of opening to
night breezes and clearing out the heated
greenhouse gases built up from every day's
blistering sun. Which is why I, for one, had come
to prefer the middle of the evening, hot as it
also was.

When I wasn't watching, that dark priest slipped
Away—glided, into one of those other planes,

I suppose; his bald head and goatee and florid shirt
hidden from me as he flattened out into
two dimensions.

One fewer than we know, or feel; where the
tension slips away, only because
the world becomes
a little less
real.

Where there are no knots - Gordian, or not.
For, to make superstrings into tangled things
requires one thread, at least, to be able to
pass over
another.

And loop back.
Perhaps *he'll* be back—
just when I lack the wherewithal
to explain all the complexities that bedevil me.
Those even higher dimensions we can't see;
but still will be—here—long after we're gone.

I'll buy him some coffee. Maybe some tea.
I'll buy him ... something. But I won't buy
his two-bit disappearing act. The pseudo-miracle,
performed by reducing his world to the
transparent, and fragile.

Unless, of course, perhaps I even sooner
shatter the glass of his mysteries.
By accident. Without meaning.

(2004)

LINGUA FRANCA

Is it not

just a semantic antic

in taxing times

to wax rhymes

about imposing

a sin tax

on syntax?

(2004)

KOAN
(Ōei 14 of Ōei gannen, or the 1,407[th] year of the *Kirishtan* Buddha)

The road was dusty, hot, and Desarimu liked to sip his tea cold by its side.

Visitors often came down the road, and Desarimu also liked the look on their grimy faces. Rivulets of sweat beaded on their skin and runneled through the dirt, though the moisture could not be wasted, and the travelers were always uncomfortable, and sometimes would even ask for a sip of tea.

A few had tried to take without asking, but Desarimu's wooden *bo* had shown them it was better, with him, to be polite.

The others, those who asked, Desarimu would often oblige, but only after drawing them into the mode of conversation Desarimu preferred. This invariably gave him an opportunity to express a profound lesson he had been working on since he was a child. And he was fifty-six years old, as of three days hence.

Wait. The next visitor was coming down the road. On foot. The heated air rising from the ground caused his image to shimmer in Desarimu's distorting vision.

The visitor kept approaching. Desarimu saw that the man wore breeches of a loose, heavy type of cloth, with leather chaps and pointed-toed boots. The man also wore a loose silk shirt, and over it all an ankle-length, leather coat. Over his shoulder was slung a simple saddle and at least forty pounds of supplies, weapons, and an armor of a type Desarimu had never before seen.

The *gaijin* wore his hair long, restrained in two places: tied into a single tail in back, with a black headband across his forehead. When the stranger neared, Desarimu tried to rivet his gaze. It was then that he noticed the *gaijin* had but one good eye.

The other eye was milky-white, obviously blinded, with a scar intersecting it from just above the brow to the lower cheek. Desarimu could not tell if the wound had been incidental to the eye's dysfunction, or the cause of it.

The man stopped, dropped his saddle and packs. He sat down roughly opposite Desarimu and said nothing. Desarimu kept his lips tight, determined not to be the first one to speak.

"You are Desarimu the monk," the *gaijin* said matter-of-factly, not seeming to mind that it was he who was required to break the silence.

"Yes," Desarimu said after a pause.

"I thought so."

The stranger quieted again. An hour passed as they sat. As though finally convinced Desarimu would not offer him tea, which was true but something Desarimu thought showed crude impatience anyway, the stranger pulled a leather wineskin from his saddle-pack. He opened the top and began to drink. Desarimu's nose crinkled ever so slightly as he smelled the same, obscure mixture of herbal and green teas he thought he, and only he, drank.

The *gaijin* paused, swallowed with gusto. He held out the skin. "Want some?" he said with a prosaic expression that Desarimu now was finding insolent.

"I have my own," he replied, trying to hide a scowl he knew was unbecoming.

The stranger shrugged. "That is good."

He finished his tea, never pausing to sip or dispense any ritual convention Desarimu could determine, gulping until the skin was empty. Then they sat, the *gaijin* stretching and sighing, and resting, for close to another hour.

"Well?" Desarimu finally demanded.

"Well what?"

"Aren't you going to ask me something about Zen?"

"Do you want me to ask you something about Zen?"

Desarimu snorted. As if this were the proper exchange!

He poured a cup full of tea, and said, "Watch."

"Hmmm?" the stranger said, apparently more interested in the interlocking rust and grey of the sunset.

"I said *watch*," Desarimu repeated himself, louder, growing irritated. He continued to pour tea into the cup. The light green liquid started to spill over the lip of the cup in a thin film.

Desarimu smiled inwardly, but forced his outward countenance to remain impassive. He had done this before, and the pilgrims always asked him why he continued to pour though the cup was full.

Desarimu continued to pour. The stranger's eyebrow cocked over his milky eye and he said nothing. The gaze of the other eye seemed to wander to the distance, attentive to nothing but the multicolored horizon, until Desarimu ran out of tea.

Finally, the *gaijin* opened his mouth to speak, still looking elsewhere.

"Why—"

"Yes, my son?" Desarimu interrupted, his eagerness betraying him.

"Why do you hold an empty kettle over a full cup as if you were pouring tea?"

Desarimu blinked. A stray thought tickled the rear of his mind that perhaps this question could have opened the door for him to say to something profound, something other than he expected; but Desarimu had no such reply, neither rehearsed nor at hand.

"You are not supposed to ask that."

"Oh," the *gaijin* said. "I am sorry." Then he sat, in silence, for a while longer.

"You were supposed to ask why I continued pouring when the cup was full!"

The stranger sighed, pursing his lips and nodding. In a mechanical voice he said, "Why did you continue to pour when the cup was full?"

Quelling the quiver in his chest, Desarimu steadied his voice and replied. "To show you that if you are like this cup, so full of your own preconceptions, then nothing new can go in. I cannot teach you about Zen until you empty your cup."

"Oh," the stranger said. He paused, then added, "I would like to buy one of these miraculous cups, that hold no air until they hold tea."

Desarimu felt the heat in his cheeks. For a moment his glance spilled to his *bo* staff. He found his hand inching toward it, nervously, when the *gaijin* spoke again, saying, "Hand your kettle to me."

The monk, apprehensive but excited, sensing a new opportunity, handed the stranger his kettle. He saw the *gaijin* unsheathe his sharp *tanto* knife and felt an instinctive, adrenalized surge. It was the kind of reaction from which Desarimu thought his studies had rendered him free. And Desarimu felt shame, and fear—at the shame and fear.

Desarimu had studied diligently, and mastered his martial arts well under the tutelage of his own Zen instructor. The man had rightly praised Desarimu at his proficiency, and who was Desarimu to question his master's opinion? Though, of course, after dispatching countless monks over the years who had been trained in a school similar to his own, the old man had died in his first scuffle with an unschooled attacker.

A teenage ruffian no less, who had simply rushed into the old man, caused him to slip in the mud and hit his head on a rock. The old man had been in their monastery's secret, undefeatable stance too; and, incidentally, had been in the process of executing their secret, undefeatable death-blow. But, of course, for the mud.

The stranger did not seem to threaten Desarimu with the knife, however. Instead, the *gaijin* touched the blade to his own forearm. He then cut into his arm; not a deep wound, but one that bled well, nonetheless. He then dribbled his blood into the teapot, and bound the wound with a clean cloth and a white, greasy salve that Desarimu assumed was antiseptic.

Then the *gaijin* opened a second wineskin of his own and emptied the full contents, Desarimu's own blend of teas again, into the kettle. Mixing the contents with a small stick, the *gaijin* then tipped the kettle toward Desarimu so that its contents, a dark red liquid that looked almost black in the interior of the kettle, were clearly visible.

The *gaijin* tipped the kettle, and its contents poured into Desarimu's green tea-filled cup. At first the new, thicker, blood-dark fluid swirled intricately into the old tea. Then the whorls expanded, dissipated, just as the cup's fluids again spilled over its lip. The old tea and the blood-darkened tea continued to mix. The stranger kept pouring. The cup kept overflowing.

By the time he had emptied the kettle, the darkness of the bloodstained, new tea had displaced all of the old, and the cup had never been emptied in the interim.

The stranger rose. He slung his belongings over his shoulder and started to walk away.

Desarimu rose quickly and ran, as fast as he could, in front of the *gaijin*, throwing himself at the stranger's feet. "Master!" Desarimu said in a high, cracking voice. "Teach me!"

The *gaijin* knelt and dropped one saddle-bag. He gently took Desarimu's hand.

Then the warrior unsheathed the *tanto* again, fed it into Desarimu's grip, and guided Desarimu's hand

until the blade barely touched the monk's other
wrist, just firm enough to be shy of making the cut.

The *gaijin*'s words echoed in Desarimu's head
long after the stranger had turned away, and
walked back up the road from which he came.

"Perhaps when you empty your cup."

—from *One Pause*

BETWEEN THE STARS

The heat came back again today.

Reminding me of when the World

was new.

Reminding me of how

under penetrating rays,

and in acid pools,

and pierced, by lightning strikes,

Life emerged.

Emerged in adversity.

Thrived, on adversity.

Grand molecules: Self-

assembling, Self-

reproducing. Self-

expressing.

Yet still, somehow, so dependent

on each other, in that trembling, slippery,

uncertain friction. That creative tension

between Self and Other, that *is* Life.

I come from a much colder place.

A place where I'd stand in the snow,

in the season that was best to view the Sky,

my own solitary breath clouding the lenses

I've needed to see, since

I was a child. Looking up,

with even more lenses,

trying to cross the spaces

between the stars.

I broke my telescope,

one of those winter nights,

under Northern Lights.

Cranked down too hard

on the tripod screw, trying

to come to focus.

Cranked down too hard

on the tripod, and the porous metal

of the fork, made brittle

by frigid air, cracked.

Rendering my grandmother's

most precious Christmas gift ever to me

useless.

I never thought, never dreamt,

I'd move to so much hotter a place,

where the sun seems to takes up the Sky.

But even this place has its seasons.

Its winter. Its spring.

And there's a spring all right

In a young woman's bounding gait

In this coffeehouse as she leaps

To serve me hot java, or cool, black tea.

In the corner, I see a younger stellar pair,

Teaching each other chess.

But all, to me, reflections

of a distant sun.

A flame-haired beauty, light-years away.

But binding me with a gravity

Einstein knew too well, yet even he

could not put

to an equation.

The heat came back today.

Reminding me of when

the World was new.

Reminding me there really was

a time, when I believed.

I could cross the spaces,

between the stars.

(2004)

CONTRA DICTION

She has this logic class.

And on the phone I ask:

Is it a paradox, or a tautology,

that Life is short;

but when it's not,

it's long?

And she questions the relative

merits of waiting

for glue to dry.

Not knowing how I

adhere, to her every point.

Search for any sign

I may have caused

her a contented sigh.

Reconceiving every lull, as

 a pregnant pause.

Across

all the electric, and magnetic

lines that bind us,

with more

than words.

(2004)

DISTANT SUN

They say I shouldn't look

into the Sun.

They say I'll go blind.

But I find that the light,

low in the horizon, that

daily threatens my vision

is an imposter.

My Sun rises and sets

too far away. Today,

for instance, I can

only see Her with

my inner vision.

And it is there that

nothing the fiery circle

that tries to blind me

can threaten.

For my Sun opens my eyes.

Staring into her doesn't blind me;

and if I look away, sooner

than I might, it's only my lack

of bravery, disguising itself

as the cause of action.

An attraction so profound,

its gravity threatens

my fragile illusions of

autonomy, and I fear

she'll suck me into

higher dimensions of reality

than I can bear.

But even there,

if I could just get over

the fear ...?

"Some studies, " it says here

"make it clear that if a man

and a woman gaze into each others'

eyes for more than seven

seconds they're either going

to kill each other

or make love."

My stopwatch is out.

Should I fear for my life;

or, looking within, find

an after-image I can't be

rid of, and rise above?

They say I cannot

touch the Sun.

They say I'll burn up.

But it's the turning, twisting

fire, the solar prominences

that inspire my every word—

whether or not heard

when I hurl them from

every spire I can find—

that consumes me the more

the further away I hide.

Even if I'm destined

only to dance across

Her surface, I'll always seek

deeper purpose. Dream of

what kindles the forces beneath,

a fraction of which is all

we'll ever see. I'll seek

everything; seek more,

even if her inaccessible core

forever remains a mystery

to me.

But the boiling Sea that washes

over the surface of two-thirds

of me, currents driven

relentlessly by the touch

of even part of Her energy,

that cannot hide.

Not any more. That door,

like my eyes, has been

thrown wide.

They say I cannot

look into the Sun.

They say I'll go blind.

But I find,

even to my constant

surprise, over and again,

what "they" say

is Nothing

but a lie.

For I'll die

when I stop

looking.

(2004)

A HOLE IN THE FIRMAMENT

What would have happened had he not been there, John wondered. Where would she have sat, that woman who wore a man's musk cologne rather than perfume, a fragrance that was also his brand?

It was a familiar aroma mingled with the unfamiliar scent of her. She smiled at him as if forgiving him that thought and butted in front of him in line.

He weighed all his options of what kind of reply to make, until it was too late to make any. Thus they met, strangers at a deli cafe, trying to get in from the rain.

When his turn came to order she was still waiting for her own order to arrive. She critiqued his choice. A Reuben? Here, she said, it was better to ask for one's corned beef without the kraut. John grunted assent and turned away, straight into the line of sight of the deli clerk who, having overheard her suggestion, asked John if he now wanted the special order instead.

To John's confusion he added the special was the Reuben without kraut. John gave him a fast, too-irritated "no," then quickly glanced away, embarrassed at how strong his reaction had been when he thought he simply wanted to be left alone.

Barely visible in his peripheral vision, he saw the corner of the woman's mouth turned up in a half-smile that sent warmth through his chest, and by reflex he almost opened his mouth to respond. Almost. Instead, when his order came, he scurried away.

Outside the rain poured and the gloss-black, wrought-iron furniture where they might have otherwise ignored each other sat empty under limp umbrellas outside storefront windows. Inside, however, there was only one table left free, so John and the woman, neither actually asking for permission from the other, shared it.

It was there they sat in what John considered an accidental configuration, until he realized that the accident never would have been repeated. And there a few members of the crowd heard the singular, faint, barely audible, and never-explained crack of the small-caliber gun, the kind whose bullets punched twenty-two-hundredths-of-an-inch diameter holes through things like plate-glass windows, and oddly attractive women.

***

John smelled ammonia. Or something else, perhaps even stronger, used here to make the hospital corridor sterile, and probably responsible for its blinding, snow-hued white. He came along on the ambulance ride when the paramedic asked him if he wanted to, and almost by reflex John said yes. The paramedic, not knowing better, must have thought John knew her. Such, John thought, were the repercussions of doing anything without thinking, especially responding to questions in the affirmative.

After the ring of the shot John had knelt over her and stayed with her. What else could the paramedic have thought? "Hi, I'm Mary," the woman said weakly from the gurney as John accompanied her down the ER hall, as if she were obligated to introduce herself after what they had been through. She extended a clammy, too-pale hand, the skin no longer seeming ivory but just pallid. John first took it in his own hand to shake, but instead held it gently, palm down, as if he meant to kiss it, only to close his other hand over the top.

The paramedic saw the gesture and pulled her away through a doorway for hospital personnel only, softly saying "I'm sorry, we will have to take her now. Wait here." What if I don't want to wait? John thought. But now there was no way that he could leave; even though, ironically, there was no way she could follow him if he did.

Ammonia. Maybe bleach. Maybe both. For a long time after, John struggled to discern the scent of the distinctive cologne behind the harsher smells, but the stretcher had long dragged the musk behind a wall of pale, blue curtains. An hour later a doctor in green scrubs finally came out from behind those curtains. "Are you Mr. Rye?" he asked John. John stammered without answering. "Are you Mr. Rye?" the physician repeated.

John suppressed a mirthless chuckle, not as successful holding back the trickle of a melancholic tear. "Rye? No," he said, clearing his throat. The hair of the doctor's mustache seemed to stand on end as his upper lip stiffened. He spun on his heel and grunted, making John realize for the first time how noncommittal the sound was, now that it was directed at him.

When John got coffee in the waiting lounge he could feel scalding warmth right through the porcelain of the mug, and thought it would burn his hands. Later, with half the bitter drink left and all of it tepid, he still felt the warmth, but only as a memory, as an absence. He wondered if he should finish the coffee, or bother getting more.

A nurse came out. John sipped quickly, realizing it was a way to look down and avoid facing the nurse's gaze. "Are you Mr. Rye?" he asked.

"No," John said firmly.

"Oh," the nurse said, seeming slightly offended. Another forty-five minutes later John was asked for a third time.

As soon as that nurse left John decided to find out what happened to Mary, to see her if possible, to smell her no matter what. The quiet buzz of a flat-line EKG beat him, coming his direction long before he could cross the curtains.

Down the hall, the words "Code blue!" fluttered, then grew in intensity, in tandem with the nearing thud of rubber-soled shoes. Then the emergency room personnel passed him, and their sounds grew more faint again.

An orderly came along much later to move the body, and John was still standing alongside the gurney, holding Mary's cold fingers in his. "I've come for her, Mr. Rye," the orderly said. Warmth flooded John's cheeks and he started to whirl angrily and deny being her husband, deny staying beside her, even deny being in the cafe, only he found himself unable to let go of her hand.

AFTER THE EXODUS

In Exodus there is

this "Pillar of Fire,"

but it's in the Valley

of Fire I find I've come to rest;

and the best thing to think

about here is how I can see,

someday,

all the flames, all the names

in the burning panoply come

here too to smolder,

eventually;

to the same place. Pouring,

like turbulent waters,

in fast floods, then slow

trickles; sneaking into

underground streams, yet

finally

to the same point in Space.

Yet in and among the faces,

the Truth I face is

that I still wait, and wait

most, for You.

(2006)

RESURRECTING OPHELIA

Adieu: c.1374, from O.Fr. adieu, from phrase a dieu (vous) commant "I commend (you) to God," from a "to" (from L. ad) + dieu "God," from L. deum, acc. of deus "god," from PIE *deiwos (see Zeus). Originally said to the party left; farewell was to the party setting forth.

Adieu, my love.

Much ado.

I watched Hamlet again today, with you.

I watched it, as if for the first time. Perhaps I did watch it, for the first time.

Seven Brides for Seven Brothers. Six Mules for Sister Sara. Five Lords-a-Leaping. Christmas, in the Bronx. Miracle, on 42nd Street.

I'd never been to the Bronx. Never been to 42nd Street.

Been to Glasgow, though. Scotland, and Montana. Iceland. South Florida, and San Francisco, and Santa Fe.

Places of loss. Los Alamos. Las Vegas.

Something must have happened to me in Vegas. I stayed.

Until I left.

At the moment, writing this—when "I" *was* writing this—on the way to Rhode Island.

Been to Rhode Island twice already. Before this. Well, more than twice if you count how many times over and back that state line to Massachusetts.

Over and back. Like that life I begun anew this morning.

Consciousness coming back, the stream, after the blankness of sleep, repaired after being broken the prior night.

Funny, you don't often think of a stream as something that breaks. You think of it as liquid. But liquid can be frozen. Even some scientists—or are they really philosophers?—conjecture that matter is frozen light.

Even light can be frozen.

But not Time. (Not something that may not …
even … really … exist.)

Was the person, the consciousness in "my" body
yesterday, was it me? Or did "I" die, when "my"
stream of consciousness broke, and when another
whirlpool of thought formed, when I woke, it just
somehow inherited nearly all of him?

Relatively speaking. But that I'm the soul of
anyone I know about, anyone who's left a trace.

Caesar, and my grandmother. Any of my one-time
loves, and Christ. I am all of them, in part.

Just so much more so the man who died last night,
who bore the same name as the me of today.

The man who thinks himself resurrected.

Thinks himself anew.

Thinks himself, then will say adieu.

Tonight, adieu. I'll say goodbye, to him, and you.
Adieu. So much ado.

To sleep. Perchance to dream, until even the dream
dies. To dream, awhile, I pray, a last dream of you.
Remember me when you watch Hamlet again
tomorrow.

Remember me, even as we watch it, for the first time.

(Adieu.)

(2005)

FREE ENERGY

Bodhisattvas ... Bolsheviks... Buddhas ....

Christ.

"Messiahs ... Mystics ... Socratics ... Sophists ..." Penny said to herself as she scanned the primary list on the view-screen. Each entry promising her a secondary list if she wanted more.

More what?

More *information.*

Penny blinked.

Blinking was not absolutely necessary to call up the menu. But Penny's condition hadn't restricted her yet to only cybernetic controls and manipulating search parameters with eye-movements felt good. Made her feel physical. Made her feel… more than just a brain in a vat.

Or technically a free-floating pod, just a castaway consciousness not-even-tossed in a droll and peaceful sea of near-Nothing where you could

429

realize both consciousness and peace were …
overrated.

But every action risked what might happen by way
of its equal and opposite reaction. Her choice
based on fighting the feeling of isolation made that
isolated feeling …

Grow.

Then Penny winced at her own thought and the
idea of "growth," and an unintentional blink made
her original reference-search go madly awry.

***

Shit. Now she had to use up precious ergs to get
back to where she had just been.

Growth. She did not really grow. Not anymore.
She staved off ungrowth. She staved off Entropy.
She staved off the inevitable.

She survived.

The word "survive" dogged her. With what
survival entailed.

More than the bionics, of course; the bionics that
she had started interfacing with three hundred
years ago, according to an Earth-calculated

reference frame. One percent of that, maybe, according to how she felt. And none of it adjusted for the temporal flux caused by Penny's ambient momentum and its path through a shifting space-time, that itself shifted because of her and her path.

And with no one else outside the pod—not here, not there, not anywhere any more—whose could tell her any other frame of reference, be it by physics or by their opinion, mattered?

"Physics" itself—or the mathematics of it— breaking down. Worse than what they'd once worried about with singularities. Those themselves bouncing in and out of nothingness to Planck distances, so that even when you calculated along correct Hypercube protocols, the space-time fluctuations yielded non-linearities.

"Even when you…" But there was no you, Penny thought. There is only Me.

She occasionally was tempted to run the equations anyway, even though they were so complex they would have utilized nearly all her computing power—and her remaining free energy.

But that could wait. If she ever wanted to finally end it all that mode of suicide was still open.

***

She just floated. Waited. A desperate woman fearing death. "Life" complicated enough at the present.

The present? When was that again?

You always could calculate it.

And die seeking to understand its Complexity. Cheeky ouroborous. Feedback loop upon feedback loop.

Those pleasant little *non-linearities.* What a sharp, merciless little irony, Penny thought, that so soon after Earth-humans had started taking "Chaos Theory" seriously they had had to face the biggest possible version of it. Not fractals in flower petals, or even hurricanes driven by a subtle butterfly wing-flap. Acceleration out of control on the scale of the universe.

Ever since the study of cosmology had started to evolve, serious discussions cropped up about how the universe would meet its End: in "fire" or "ice?" (Thank you, Robert Frost.) Would the universe continue indefinitely in the expansion started by the Big Bang—and the "heat death" that allowed none of the spread out energy to flow and no machine, mechanical or digital or biological, to run? Or was there enough mass in the Universe, so that gravity between objects eventually slowed it down and pulled it back in a "Big Crunch" that destroyed everything ordered or living in the pressure?

Heat Death had won. Whoopee.

But once upon a time, everyone from the poorest bum on the street who might have heard of the primal quandary of universal fate to the wildest-haired professor took solace in one fact, that either way, the absolute version of The End would not occur for billions of years from their own time. They would be dead long before they ever saw it.

That was what the calculations said. Calculations of the dynamics of the universe's expansion. Trajectories.

Ah, yes, Penny tried to suppress the grimacing cackle she felt rise in what was left of her throat. *Trajectories*. The very things Chaos Theory indicated were usually rational and predictable, but always pregnant with the unexpected twist.

There had been the surprises of dark matter (or the illusion that didn't exist, she laughed) and dark matter (the illusion that didn't even not exist). There had been Planck bounce, and topo-inversion. Sometimes the best calculations were only off a little on their basic parameters, but when "a little bit off" entered a feedback loop *trajectories* could take off wildly in a direction no one expected.

Like the fact that a rate of universal expansion that seemed regular for billions of years could be accelerating. But more, that the rate of acceleration *itself* could be accelerating.

And all of it end in a mere thirty-three "years."

Penny "sat" down to what might be the last meal synth-meal the Recyclotron could offer. All that remained of her body was a minimum array of essential organs, in the minimal necessary structural components of head and torso. All musculoskeletal function had been slowly taken over by bionics. Over time, with free energy reserves growing lower and lower, Penny had to finally admit the cybernetic implants in her brain were enough to command the module, and her movement within the pod served no purpose but helping her pass the time.

The redundant bionics had been "recycled." Penny only had to go through two mental breakdowns before she became used to being interface-restricted.

The meal smelled good. Which made her wish to retch the more. But her stomach was empty, and she ate the food that the capsule controls magnetically levitated into her mouth.

Some of it might even have been Andy.

"Take and eat, for this is My body…"

***

No, she thought, relaxing in the sated aftermath. The charade of a roast prime rib was not Andy. Which was nice, when she thought of the wickedly painful yet hilarious blasphemy of her quoting Communion when it just as well could refer to how many times she'd given Andy a blowjob. And the funny turning back to sad when she thought of how often he'd begged her to swallow when she wouldn't.

I loved you.

But if anything of what she'd eaten was him, he couldn't hear. Even anything "karmic" about him was being lost, as the information, the patterns, that had defined him were broken down and leeched of their nutritive value. He'd been recycled innumerable times, like countless detritus the pod itself encountered in its passive, random momentum.

Her right arm. The oxygen gauge.

Her own shit.

It wasn't Andy. The more she survived—the more she ate whatever was left to eat—the more anything of him that lived on lived on only in her own brain.

Almost without doubt a bit of the prime rib had been Andy, she admitted, finally. But she could not let him go to waste, now could she?

***

Later (how much later? She had no idea) Penny woke from a tornadic but unremembered dream— raging in part because she knew whatever was lost of the dream was probably lost forever—roaring silently in something between laughter and weeping. Silently; her larynx, an unnecessary accouterment in a place where there was no one else to hear her, had long since been fed to the Recyclotron. Tears poured from her eyes, with the excess moisture automatically also sucked in and *integrated*.

Body heat. Simple molecular form. Not much energy value, but some. Treated to the right quantum-catalytic processes.

What a groundbreaking discovery it would have been, in the normal world of her childhood, had physicists not needing to be driven by terrified fear of brute survival found it earlier. Just how much free energy could be wrung from tears.

Para-matter. Namalk reactions. The dicey time being the start; catalyzing the process and kick starting a Namalk reaction took about a couple hundred trillion ergs of reserves. Only with the proportionally paltry payoff of about a couple hundred million ergs in return, on top of the original couple hundred trillion investment. If something went wrong the loss…

But if it didn't. A couple hundred million ergs someone might otherwise not have.

Even more than the recycling of her excrement, the violation of her tears in the name of survival made Penny's gorge rise. She cybernetically commanded the plate to be levitated and thrown into the Recyclotron. Bits of artificial roast beef still stuck to it. Then they were sucked in too.

Penny felt sorry for those remnants of reconstructed-organic material. Sorry because what remained of her own "organic material" would be gone too. Soon.

That was the way of things. No matter how relative "soon" could be.

***

Penny's mouth hurt. Too dry. The climate controls in the capsule had fluctuated; it was not merely her imagination at work. She looked at the gauges. The power levels read low again.

She wondered if she had been lax in monitoring them. That would be funny. She had never been negligent at any job she had held on Earth; first cashiering, then a fast food sandwich jockey, finally social work. Before the universe's ... "little problem."

Thirty-three years, to her. And back then the world, both the one in general and hers, had felt so overburdened. Not even just with the real specters of overpopulation and climate change, pollution, and war and famine. Everyone in their own personal sphere "just getting by." Or saying that to themselves.

Even then there were prophets of Entropy-doom. Penny snorted a chuckle. They had no idea of the scale of the problem coming their way, within their own lifetime.

At first the weirdness came by astrophysical data from long-range radio-telescope arrays. What a joke; they had been SETI devices set out to look for patterned communications from extraterrestrial sentients. But the deviations in the universe's expansion were slight. It had to be some curiosity without threat, or even a hoax.

But then it was dark matter, so long a darling of astrophysical explanation after long before that being thought a joke, that was revealed at the hoax. Dark energy too, but not the force for expansion attributed to it. The cosmological constant that wasn't necessarily constant.

Hyperinflation indeed. Except the shocking discoveries said there had been no hyperinflation in the universe's earliest moments. The calculations were a bit off. The hyperinflation was about to happen now.

Exponentially increase.

You soon could look through a backyard telescope to take in the sad beauty of the stars blinking out even as you watched.

But necessity is the mother of invention. And in this case the discovery of para-matter. Namalk reactions. Quantum catalysis.

So had started the boom industry to build the capsules. The pods.

Suddenly those same people to whom a few hundred million had been a waste, when it came to manned space travel, wanted trillions of dollars poured into pod-development. And all the while the measured acceleration of the Universe's expansion gave not only increasing, but wildly fluctuating values.

Terrifying. In purely rational terms it should have given slight, if only slight, glimmers of hope. But in the reality of being human, not knowing when or how one was to die generated even more panic.

No need to fear overpopulation, when people fought each other over pods, or iPods or food or drink or sex or anything else they now deemed valuable at the moment if they had accepted death and insisted on going out with appetites indulged, until ten billion had bloodied themselves down to a few million in a handful of years.

Penny had eaten, and drank herself numb, and fucked a lot. But she was most focused on the pods. Oh, Penny knew pods. Her only steadfast relationship among all the fucking was one of the first and best pod-men.

Andy's designs came out so far ahead of everyone else's technology that he finally decided he wasn't going to share them with anyone, anymore. Except Penny.

Maybe Mother was right. Penny should have married him. What a provider.

Her mother had always said, before all the madness: *"he would make such a good father."*

Penny's mother had died before the coming Heat Death was discovered, but she still knew how to speak. Through the good old-fashioned encoding of Penny's synapses, her still-as-of-now-intact head and brain, just as the ghosts of countless mothers in countless millennia of human existence had spoken to their daughters. But Penny's mother could speak too, even if it was a waste of free energy, through a perfect simulacrum popped into Penny's brain through the data in the pod's information-banks.

Not a memory. Too clear and sharp to even confuse with one. An entirely recreated *experience.*

Part of the benefits of quantum catalyzing through para-matter using Namalk reactions. A by-product discovered was that the intimate relationship between things like free energy and entropy in thermodynamics and the analogous concepts in information theory was a reality. Any matter that gave itself up to have its free energy used had all the information associated with it through the history of the universe not destroyed but put into a stasis that was accessible.

If one simply was willing to use an obscene amount of *other* free energy to access it.

Which grabbed and stored in stasis even more information.

Ghosts. You could resurrect any ghost, perfectly. So long as you were willing to sacrifice a new ghost to do it.

Always wondering if the new one screamed in stasis, waiting to be resurrected. Asking when the sacrifice to raise it from the dead would come. When it would be his or her turn.

Life, Penny, thought. Reality's first Ponzi scheme.

***

Penny didn't need to waste huge amounts of free energy to hear a resurrected mother pine for grandchildren. Why? To see them die?

To see Recyclotrons devour them as their capsules fought each other to feed on a few scraps of free energy?

Oh, yes, Andy's design had been the best. With tears streaming down Penny's face whose free energy her pod eagerly sucked up and recycled for her she remembered how each of their capsules had eaten many a screaming child.

Yes, Mama. Andy would have made such a good father.

The only thing he wasn't that good at was monitoring gauges.

His pod broke down next to Penny's. And her Recyclotron, just like his, was always hungry.

But I had been asleep. So maybe he never even screamed.

At least she'd never heard him.

Penny returned to the data-stores and started scrolling again. In it one would find the key ideas from a number of seminal-thinking scientists, mostly Earth-born, which were necessary for continuing function and repair of Penny's pod. Besides the entire run of *I Love Lucy*.

She had disciplined herself to only one representational piece of "pure" entertainment at a time. But she also had felt compelled to save every utterance of every Earth-philosopher and theologian, and even a few from other worlds, dating from the universe's beginning.

Every utterance. Every damned *thought*, though some of them took so much effort—and energy— to access, that Penny disdained the attempt.

Just food.

She especially liked calling up and tormenting the Plato simulacrum. Seeing him struggle with the fact that there was no transcendent reality of Mind. Not if all matter and energy was information and information was mind—and yet also could be no more than food. Mind was malleable, spirit could be translated and passed on from one medium to another, but it was always, somehow, *embodied.*

In any knock-down, drag-out between atoms and axioms, atoms won. Not because they *were* superior. Just because they were free of the illusion they were.

Penny at least could forgive Aristotle. In the best way possible, perhaps. Letting him stay silent, and dead.

He was so much closer but would have been tormented anyway too. Add the quantum games and even embodied logic was slippery; binary code was great at slipping straitjackets just enough to make resurrections perfect but prediction still as impossibly full of potential errors as that old belief the universe had billions of years left.

Existence still preceded essence. Thanks, Jean-Paul.

Have you met my friend, Recyclotron?

Yet even Recyclotron was not immortal.

Soon, like the other equipment placed in the maw of the ominous machine in the corner of the pod, the latest information she had accessed would be leftover, dark para-matter. Integrated into the capsule. With a few modifications the pod had been able to take the para-matter and structure it quite nicely around the hull. Now it was a fine, spiderweb-lattice around the pod; perfect for snaring even the measliest of free-floating particles to feed the Recyclotron.

From food, to shit.

Man did not live by bread alone. But by every erg that proceeded from the mouth of Recyclotron.

She laughed.

It was better than screaming.

She had screamed too much lately. Some variety was called for.

***

Penny woke. Or assumed she did, unable to tell much from the look out the window of the capsule. Out, into dark, empty space. Still no stars, of course. Burned out long ago. *Blinked.* Her pod's gauges did the same, though their light did not go out. She checked to see what had alarmed the pod's sensor array.

Oh. Now wasn't *this* interesting?

Wicked, wicked little non-linearities. Gremlin, cackling little non-linearities.

Goblin, troll, growing like magic non-linearities.

According to her gauges, while she slept the Universe's rate of expansion had slowed.

Now ... under her very observation ... stopped.

Reversed.

The destabilizing effect of her own para-matter lattice? Had it collected enough matter to give the gravity profile of the Universe a new perturbation?

Was this a good thing?

Her energy gauges roared to life, first flickering and then going wild with explosively rising levels, as the universe that was previously expanded so close to Heat Death now contracted wildly. Brought her ever more matter on which to feed, with almost more free energy than she could bear.

Enough to access and re-create more and more simulacra, as fast as she could desire it.

And Penny had never been good at resisting temptation.

The sensor array was blank.

Where was she?

Where Penny had been but a mote in the expanding universe, what was *she* in the contracting one?

Would she be immense in spatial terms, or did space-time's collapse negate such questions?

And why, with such a collapse, were things still so dark?

Was she a black hole now? A singularity? The gravity in such an object should have torn her apart. Yet ... could it tear her apart if she had never fallen into it? If instead it had formed around her?

Was her?

A God.

... still with no Answers.

Give in to it.

It felt good.

Give in to it.

It hurt.

Like no other sensation she had ever felt before.

Like every sensation ever possible.

Penny thought it strange, that she saw and smelled and heard with devices that sensed not only visible light and molecular particles to quantum flickerings and rarefactions of quark fields. She had always known what the monitors could do. She just had never wondered how they would *feel*.

Was I just born? she thought. Am I just now alive?

I can't seem to remember anything. Well, some things. Bits and pieces.

You don't want children? someone snarled.

Children, Penny thought? She was just new born; how could babies have children?

He would have made a good father.

Who, she thought, who would have made such a good Father? There was no one here, and she was alone.

The loneliness burned. She felt caressed by little things, other … *souls*. Brushing against the metallic skin of her expanded body. The universe's few remaining particles, tumbling into the singularity. Into her.

The little souls joining her seemed scarcely alive, and they little better company than pets. She ate them. They tasted good, and did not mind too much being eaten, but they did not fill her.

So she started to eat herself.

Not all. Only the unnecessary parts.

She could see forward as well as backward in Time.

Not Space. Where was there Space? What was Space? Everything crunched down.

Everything felt so claustrophobic. She had no room. What happened to her space?

"I'm leaving you, George. I need my space."

"Bull. You're leaving me for this Andy!"

Well, why not? He'd make such a good Father.

I'm hungry, Mama.

Baby, Mama don't eat don't nobody eat.

There were now only tiny pets to eat.

They came more intermittently, and had little energy for her, and small minds. But Penny ate them, and she stretched, and there was no room.

Called out for someone, when no one answered.

Only her little pets, and she ate them.

She ate them, until she had eaten the last one, and space had crunched down totally, and she was alone.

Still hungry.

Yet surrounded by live ghosts.

There was dear Friedrich, and his Eternal Return. And look—there was that little Sakyamuni! Such a cute little sophist.

Then there were those impatient with sophists; there, the Big Three: Ari, and the Pug-face, and the Forehead.

Vain, vain, all so vain.

And yet in such pain.

Wanting to live.

And Penny could do it. Make them live again.

At the quantum level they were defined, finite in scope. Even the entire collection of particles and dynamics they had been from birth to death was finite. She had the power. She could resurrect them.

She could cry out and tear herself apart in an explosive Creation, and bring them back, all of them, happy and whole!

Couldn't she?

What was wrong, Penny wondered. A stab of pain tore through what felt like her side.

What was missing?

Perfect knowledge. Near perfect she had. But not perfect.

"The gap between near-infinity and infinity is still an infinity…"

Thanks a lot, Mr. Roberts, you prickish middle school pedant.

Slight differences in initial conditions.

Wild changes in trajectories.

What could she not know, and know perfectly, when she could know Everything?

(Myself …)

She could Create All.

But She could not bring them back.

Powerless, irretrievable echoes. And herself as well. Hidden, wholly irretrievable echoes, in a new universe.

She could make it. A new reality. So much like the old one that others very much like her and all the ones she'd known and now knew would live. But no one would live again. And when the new universe died, another—probably almost the same—would evolve to live. But when it too died, no one would really live again.

Cycle upon cycle. Hiding a near-infinity of pained, irretrievable echoes. Ghosts incapable of even haunting their house.

It's not worth it ..., she said to herself. It's not worth it.

And She could end it.

She could end the cycle of (life) death. She could end the cycle of (love) pain. She could end this.

Stay here, lone guardian of a forever-silence. With one word (*no!*) she could make sure they hurt no more.

(No!)

It was not worth it.

(No!)

Penny resolved to free them.

(No!)

She would affirm that lone, rebel word.

No.

But though She knew all, she did not know herself.

And somehow the Word she whispered, or thought, or screamed, was yes.

Yes I said yes I will.

Yes.

SOMEWHERE NORTH OF SLO (San Luis Obispo)

White, and smooth, as bleached bone,

the driftwood comes to be at home,

on this beach, signaling it's out of reach

of strife, signaling it's done with its prior life:

with all demands of desiccating salt, and shoals,

and surf, as much with any challenges of Earth,

of its roots, trying to remain grounded in the face

of wind, or rot.

But like some lighthouse keeper on the strand—

even though I'm not—I'm tempted

to toss a match into this atomic pile,

to ignite a signal, visible for all the miles

through the fog.

But not knowing the beach

regulations in this strange state.

Not knowing, if I'll overstep

my bounds.

(2006)

CONSUMMATUS EST

I'm not finished yet.

This is a piece I'll never finish.

A piece, that

in this enclosed space,

within this boundary condition,

still spirals inward,

spirals inward,

spirals inward,

 to infinity.

But I'm not finished yet.

Not when, within

this enclosed space,

fractal boundaries surround

all we'll ever see,

spiraling ...

spiraling ...

spiraling inward ...

further than infinity can

ever be.

Per terras,
et per mare,

Ad astra,
et ad infinitum,

Amor fati.

And I'm not finished yet.

(2005)

PUBLICATION HISTORIES

"The Artifice of Respiration" and "BIOS 1.1" were first published in *Darkling Plain* #1, Winter/Spring 2001

"6367828" was first published in *Weirdbook* #26, Autumn 1991

"Excalibur" was first published in *Weirdbook* #27, Spring 1992

"The Eldest Edda" was first published in *Auk Contraire* #1, 2016

"The Shrew That Are Rush Limbaugh" and BIOS 2.2 was first published in *Tales of the Unanticipated* #20, Fall/Winter/Spring 1998-9

"One Poor Devil" was first published in *MidNight ExPress* #16, 1999

"The Tragic Death of a Small Hunger" was first published in *The Yellow Booke* vol. 1, October 2014

"The Hitch" was first published in the zine *Get Well Soon!*, 2015

"Counting Coup" was first published in *The Minnesota Daily*, poetry contest winners for Spring 1990

"Enoch," "Blaspheming," "Beauty" and "The Weeping Dragon" were first published as part of the novel *Eyes*, Xaos Books/Chaos Warrior Productions 1993

"The Year We Made Contact" was first published in *The Yellow Booke* vol. 2, October 2015

"Angel in Orion" was adapted in a short film that made its first public appearance at the 2012 Dam Short Film Festival in Boulder City, Nevada

"Autoscopy" was first published in *Auk Contraire* #2, 2017

"Koan" was first published in *Tales of the Unanticipated* #16, Spring/Summer/Fall 1996

"A Hole in the Firmament" was first published in *The Slate*, Fall 1996

"Free Energy" was first published in *Auk Contraire* #1, 2016

Additional notes: "Mourning Light" in prose is adapted from an unproduced short screenplay co-written with Ted Hall and Therese Evans, 1993

AFTERWORD

"Thirty-three years since the change?" the apparition said. "You know, that's how long Jesus was a man."

"Really? I was not aware of it."

The girl scowled. "Don't be facetious."

Those are lines from a novel I first wrote, well, almost thirty-three years ago. One that took its own convoluted road to publication in what seemed, at the time, a painfully long journey of eight years.

Little did I know that it would take so much longer to compile enough published short stories for a collection. Not that the shorts were a high priority for me, but still.

So here we finally have them. Padded out by a large number of poems as well, some of which have become fixtures over the years in the many recitation and spoken word performances I've done at various venues. Though, ironically, those rarely having been the ones that have been accepted for publication—while the ones I've been less proud of, the most "emo" ones from my earliest days, found quick homes in print. Go figure.

Then again, that was a pattern exhibited in the short stories too. For whatever reason the ones I've worked hardest on and been most proud of as having some substance and depth took the very longest to find a home, often many decades. While the more "toss off" ones found homes in print much sooner and more easily.

There's probably a lesson in there. But one I refuse to heed. Which tells most people all they'll need to know in brief about my "writing career."

My only huge regret being that I could have compiled this collection just a bit sooner. It was supposed to have come out around November or December of 2017 at the latest, but literally on the very night formatting was complete, I got a call I thought was from my father, but when I answered was from his partner of many decades. And my dad, who had grown over the adult years to become probably my best friend, was dying.

Needless to say, that threw the proverbial monkey wrench into the final proceedings of this collection, as well as a couple other works. Dad had always been my most steadfast advocate in support of my writing aims—though blessedly never one to push either, and just as supportive of me just being a writer out of love, on my own terms. Rushing back to Minnesota to see him, it was more sudden and serious than anyone there had realized. I only had time to talk to him a couple afternoons when on the third day he passed.

And in the months since, as much as part of me ostensibly burned with a "desire" to finish this all up in his memory, a frank admission would be that that drive was all cognitive, intellectual, symbolic. Without him ever being able to see the collection, there has been little visceral, emotional *oomph*, and procrastination of a sort crept in.

I can't say exactly what just barely broke that ice. But here, in the waning days of 2018, it has. And so—even a bit more than thirty-three years since the process started—you have what you see before you.

Whether it's in reality more the *terminus* of a fiction writing life or a resurrection, we'll just have to let the future unfold and see.

Or, perhaps, to quote Forrest Gump, "I think maybe it's both. Maybe both is happenin' at the same time."

Always.

ABOUT THE AUTHOR

Robert Subiaga Jr's peripatetic path has led, physically, from Minneapolis to Glasgow, Iceland to the Everglades to the Mohave Desert, the lights of Las Vegas to the Sierra Nevada and the Pacific. Armed with a B.A. in Physiology, an interdisciplinary M.A. in Liberal Studies, and a range of various teaching certifications over the years, his abstract wanderings have taken him just as many places, especially as an educator particularly working with outlier populations such as at-risk youth, and/or the highly gifted.

Subiaga was the screenwriter and executive producer of the 2005 short film **The Gnostic**, starring the late Francesco Quinn, has been a frequent fixture on various poetry and spoken word circuits, and was the author of the 1993 novel **Eyes** and—after a two decade plus hiatus from novels—2017's experimental/apocalyptic/ dystopian work **The Judgment of Helen**.

He is now at work on **The New Mystic**, a non-fiction exploration of the philosophical interrelationship of scientific realism, existential realities, and art.